Auntie Caroline's Last Case

A Bobbie Bassington Story

Bob Able

Books in this series by Bob Able:

Double Life Insurance

Bobbie And The Spanish Chap

Bobbie And The Crime-Fighting Auntie

Bobbie And The Wine Trouble

Chapter 1

In the year since she moved to Ballybunion on the Irish coast, Pauline Patrick, retired and recently widowed Legal Executive, had settled into her little cottage around the corner from the golf links hotel, and acquired a small elderly dog from a rescue centre.

The dog insisted on its walk early each morning and Pauline had devised a clever route in a figure of eight, taking in an element of the path known as the 'Wild Atlantic Way' but passing close enough to the cottage to give up and go home half way round the perimeter of the golf course section, if the dog became too tired to continue on inclement days, or when his arthritis troubled him.

The section of the walk they both enjoyed most was where the path dropped down steeply onto a sandy cove known locally as 'Ladies Beach', which was sheltered from the wind but usually deserted, at least this early in the morning.

It was on this little beach that the dog suddenly took it into its head to pull away from her and tear off down to the sea to investigate something which had obviously washed up there during the night.

Although she called repeatedly, the dog would not come away and Pauline had to trek down the sand to the water's edge, to re-capture her wilful little pet.

As she approached she saw that what was interesting the dog looked like a bundle of old clothes tied together with thin blue nylon rope. But as she got closer the bundle took on a more recognisable shape.

The body, for that is what it was, had obviously been in the water for a while, but the disturbing thing was that the wrists and ankles had been tied together at the back so that the corpse assumed a kneeling position. As the dog pulled at a bit of what looked like the hood of a raincoat, a neat round hole in the back of the almost hairless skull was revealed, which made it obvious that the cause of death was being shot in the head from behind.

Pauline fought down the urge to scream as she caught and re-attached the lead to the dog, and forced herself to stay calm as she reached into her pocket for her mobile phone and dialled the emergency services number.

-ooo0oo-

Pedro, so happy, but struggling to express himself, had memorised a passage from one of Bobbie's collection of 20th Century humorous writer's books, kept in her substantial book case, and prepared himself to recite it to her.

'Bobbie,' said Pedro, clearing his throat, 'I'm a so happy, and you are without exception the dearest, a sweetest, loveliest, most perfect and er, angelic thing that ever lived.'

'I know,' giggled Bobbie. 'Aren't you lucky?'

Pedro realised that Bobbie's response was the very next line in the passage from the book he had been committing to memory.

'Ah ...'

'A direct quote from "The Small Bachelor" by P G Wodehouse, published in 1927, if I am not mistaken ... how clever of you to learn it, Pedro!'

'Yays, but is all true, my Bobbie. I'm learned from a the book because I don't know the English words make the show how I feeling like this book, and you no speak the Spanish ...'

'Yes, Wodehouse was a rather wonderful wrangler of words, wasn't he ...'

'But he saying what I mean. What I trying to say you. I so happy Bobbie ...'

'That is so sweet, Pedro. And you learned that passage just to express your happiness?'

Pedro twisted his hands in embarrassment, and blushing deeply, mumbled an almost inaudible 'Yays.'

Kissing him on the forehead, Bobbie looked around her. They had both been so contented in the scruffy, but conveniently situated flat they rented on the Richmond Road in Kingston-on-Thames, on the outskirts of London. In the months since Rosy, Bobbie's university friend and original flatmate had moved out and Pedro had moved in, their lives had taken on a sort of gentleness which deepened their love and increased their commitment to each other daily.

Pedro was always very attentive and courteous and did his best to do his share of the chores and cleaning, especially when Bobbie was involved in her work as a trainee investigative journalist or needing to get her head down to study, particularly now that her post graduate course was coming to an end.

The only fly in the ointment of this idyll was the gradually failing health of Bobbie's Auntie Caroline who, as an established and rather well connected investigative journalist, had employed Bobbie, paid for her training, and now involved her in running her business as a partner. Caroline had been given a year to live nine months ago, and had insisted that Bobbie stayed in London to complete her course while she returned to her beloved cottage in Scotland.

Bobbie now commuted backwards and forwards between this Scottish house and London and spent as much time as she was able at her Aunt's side, learning the finer points of investigative journalism and, when her aunt was well enough, going with her to meet some of the myriad and fascinating connections she had developed over her long career. Bobbie hoped to be able to depend on some of those contacts when her aunt passed away, and when she took on sole responsibility to for the business they were building.

Following several high profile investigations, which had lead to some great press coverage and the sale of their stories through Button and Cohen, the international news agency, the business was in fine shape and now Bobbie had rather more potential stories to investigate than she could handle.

She was not very interested therefore when she received an email from her friend Henry, at the news agency, tipping her off about the discovery of a body on a beach somewhere in southern Ireland.

She forwarded the email to her aunt in case she had any comment to make, but almost immediately received a follow up email from Henry to say that the body had been identified as someone called Eoin O'Grady.

The name meant nothing to Bobbie, but she dutifully forwarded the second email to her aunt and thought no more about it.

Moments later, however, her mobile phone rang and she found that her aunt was very interested in this story indeed.

-ooO0oo-

Geoff and Janet loaded the last of the shopping into the boot of the Jaguar and Geoff held open the door for Janet to get in.

'Thank goodness that's all done,' said Geoff. 'I look forward to seeing Rosy and Bobbie and Pedro, but it would be much easier if we didn't have to cook for them.'

'We can't keep going out to restaurants, Geoff,' stated Janet. 'You know we always end up paying when Bobbie comes, and you are much to quick to offer when the bill arrives.'

'Well, I …' Geoff climbed into the car and started the engine.

'You do. You know you do. You just don't like a fuss, so you reach for your wallet before anyone gets embarrassed.'

'Perhaps you are right, love,' smiled Geoff. He had always spoilt Bobbie when she was a child and now that had rather extended to include her friends.

'I am looking forward to getting to know David a little better on Sunday though,' said Janet thoughtfully. 'And hearing about their new place in Putney.'

'Must be costing them a fortune,' said Geoff. 'Its a good job Rosy got a promotion.'

'Yes, and I think David is doing quite well at the bank, now he has finished at college.'

'Does he work with Pedro, then?'

'No, I don't think so. Same college course, different bank, as far as I can make out.'

'Well, judging by all that food in the back, they are certainly not going to go hungry.'

'Its only roast pork,' said Janet. 'You can't go wrong with a roast and a few veg. Typical Sunday fare'

'A few veg! It felt to me like you had bought the farm, carrying all those bags!'

-ooOOoo-

Bobbie was able to answer her aunt's question as to how the body was so swiftly identified following another email from the ever vigilant Henry.

His latest message explained that the authorities found a wallet with a driving licence, twenty-five euros and some credit cards in the victim's trouser pocket and a payslip in another pocket in his coat.

'Why are you so interested in this chap?' Bobbie asked.

'I've met him, albeit briefly and years ago. He was a contact who put me onto a really big story.'

'What was that?'

'You remember that night in your flat when you asked me to tell you a scary bedtime story, and I told you about what happened to me during "the troubles" in Ireland? Well he gave me the tip to meet the skipper of the boat running the guns. He was a junior crew member.'

Bobbie recalled the incident with great clarity. She had no idea until that point what dangerous situations her Auntie Caroline had found herself in before that story was told, and she remembered it almost word for word.

'On the seventh of February 1987, I was in Dublin,' Caroline had said.
'We had gone to a cinema where we planned to meet someone who said he could fix a meeting for us with Adrian Hopkins, who was the skipper of a ship that we were pretty certain was running guns from Libya to the IRA in Ireland. We were right about him, but it took almost a year for the authorities to catch him, and this was pretty much at the beginning of our investigations into his activities.'

'Guns?' Bobbie had asked in astonishment.

'Yes. I worked for a big newspaper group in those days in a team who were involved in all sorts of things. Anyway, as I was saying, we turned up at this old cinema which was all closed up and there was nobody around, so we wandered round to the back to see if our contact was

there. It was just as well we did because, as we went behind the back wall, there was one hell of an explosion that blew out the whole front of the cinema.'

'Oh, my goodness! I remember that story,' Bobbie said now. 'And that is why you had to go and live in that safe house we visited in London, isn't it.'

'Yes, pretty much. Eoin O'Grady was small fry and his tip-off didn't produce the results we were hoping for as the meeting with his boss never actually took place, but the ship he worked on, The Eksund, I think it was called, or something like that, was used to carry the biggest haul of weapons the IRA had ever tried to smuggle into Ireland, and it's capture, some time after I was due to meet the skipper, marked the moment when the powers that be realised the IRA had the finances and contacts to raise and equip what amounted to an army.'

'Blimey!'

'Maybe the Libyans or perhaps the IRA caught up with Eoin O'Grady, and maybe it was him who betrayed the gun runners. I guess we will never know, but I think we should cover this, and my previous involvement in the past may create a good story with some solid background.'

'Absolutely. I see your point, Auntie Caroline.'

'You will need to get in touch with the Irish Police and perhaps chat up the Coastguard and the person who found the body to start digging on this one, Bobbie.'

'I'm on it,' said Bobbie, as a thrill of excitement ran up her spine. She was in for a busy week.

-ooOOoo-

'Come on, you great oaf, answer the phone,' muttered Rosy.

She did not often need to contact David when he was at work, but this was something of a special case.

Having settled into their new rented home on the outskirts of Putney, David and Rosy now had the use of that much treasured local asset, a parking space, but without a car of their own had not so far used it. Now Rosy had the opportunity to put that right.

Following her recent promotion they had decided that they could afford a modest secondhand car which David could use to get to work and which would enable them to get out of London and visit Rosy's family at weekends.

Rosy tapped her foot impatiently as she listened to the ringing tone. She had an appointment at the dentist in an hour and, having taken the morning off work to attend, had spent the earliest part of the working day in a slightly dubious car 'showroom' behind a parade of shops near the tube station. There she had examined and briefly driven a superficially tidy looking Ford which they had spotted while walking past on a couple of occasions.

Inside, the car was showing its age, and although she had been assured that everything worked, Rosy had formed the impression that it had had to work hard to cover the 120,000 miles on the clock. Externally, however, it seemed to have fared slightly better and with the exception of a dent and a very obvious paintwork repair to one rear door, it looked presentable enough.

Rosy wanted to make an offer for it because the salesman had explained that the other couple who were interested in it were due to return from the bank shortly, and put down a deposit to secure it.

'Hello?' said a sheepish voice at the end of the phone.

'At last!' exclaimed Rosy. 'Where have you been?'

'Erm ... I'm in the toilet actually, Rosy. Couldn't I ring you back?'

'What! Oh you big muffin. Trust you! I'm in the car place and that blue car is alright. But I've got to hurry up and agree something if we are going to get it because the chappie has another couple coming in with a deposit shortly, and he will sell it to them if we don't do a deal straight away ...'

'Well, I'm not sure, Rosy. It is a lot of money to spend out and it has got a lot of miles on the clock ...'

'The chappie says that the average milage is 15,000 a year so, given its age its actually less than the average.

And you said yourself that it looks quite good …'

'Have you driven it?'

'Had you forgotten, David, dear, that the reason I came here to wait on their doorstep this morning was to do that very thing?'

'No, but …'

'I have been round the block, and then, because it seemed all right, around the bigger block in it, and established that the chappie will give us a three month warranty if we pay the price on the screen for it.'

'Well, I don't know … isn't there time for me to drive it as well?'

'Perhaps I have not made myself clear, cloth-head. The chappie, who is now walking towards me, by the way, has someone else coming in to buy the wretched car if we don't agree a price on it straight away. Now do I, or do I not have your permission to get a deal done?'

'I suppose so, if you are sure about this. Don't you think you could get a bit off the price, though. It seems an awful lot of money to me …'

'I will try, David. I must go now.' And with that she ended the call.

-ooo0ooo-

'Well, then you will have to go there in person,' Caroline was saying. 'How far away is this Ballybunion place?'

Bobbie explained where Ballybunion was, that she had established that the hotel on the golf links adjacent to where the body was discovered had a room at a reasonable price, and that she could fly into an airport not too far away with a budget airline.

'Ballybunion sounds a pretty unlikely name to me,' said Caroline. 'Are you sure its genuine?'

'Yes. I've checked it out. I've found out it is on what is called the 'Wild Atlantic Way,' which is a popular tourist thing, and the body was on a little beach just outside the town. The people from the hotel know the woman who found it and put me in touch, and she seems quite happy to meet me.'

'Well done, Bobbie. Better get down there as soon as you can before the press pack descends.'

'Will you be all right?'

'Of course. As it happens I've got to go over to the hospital tomorrow again and they might want to keep me in for what they call "observation" overnight, probably because they can't believe how well I'm feeling, so I will be well cared for.'

'Well, if you are sure ...'

-ooO0oo-

Kerry Airport is 37.5kms from Ballybunion, and

Ryanair deposited Bobbie on time at the terminal, where the cheapest hire car she could find on the internet would be waiting to take her to the hotel by the golf links.

A small dark haired man was waiting in the arrivals area to meet her, holding up a crumpled envelope with her name on it.

'Hello. I'm Declan,' he said as she made herself known to him. 'If you would like to follow me, I'll take you to your car.'

They walked past the desks of several of the better known car hire companies and then out into the 'Drop Off' area where people were loading and unloading passengers and luggage.

She was surprised to see that the car Declan approached was quite dirty and obviously not new.

'Is this the car?' she asked.

'Well bless you, no!' stated the little man. 'There is no room to park here at the airport so we just pick people up here and take them to the office. Its just you today, so we can get straight off, if you are ready. We are not like these big companies with desks here, that is how we keep our prices down. I took your booking on the internet myself, by the way.'

-ooo0ooo-

'How is the sprite ... er, I mean your niece ... Roberta

isn't it?' Retired Colonel Cyril Duncan-Browne asked, as he and Geoff met by chance in the baker's shop.

'Oh, hello Cyril. Yes she is fine, thanks. They are coming to dinner on Sunday and I've been sent out to round up some last minute soft drinks as her boyfriend doesn't drink.'

'Best you try Waitrose for that, old chap. This is a bakery.'

'Ah, but Waitrose don't sell these fabulous doughnuts,' Geoff held up the bag he had just purchased. 'And although, being a dentist, Janet doesn't approve, I find them irresistible.'

'Me too. I'm here to get some of those myself.'

'I understand that they are going to put some tables and chairs in here and make a little cafe area. Marvellous idea. It will become a sanctuary for the husbands and what-not while the ladies go round Waitrose, and I'm looking forward to a coffee and one of these superb doughnuts fresh from the oven when it opens.'

'Well that is splendid news, Geoff. Perhaps we could meet up in here on occasions when sent out to gather foodstuffs or visit the shops?'

'An excellent suggestion, Cyril,' smiled Geoff. 'And have you been fishing lately?'

-ooOOoo-

Chapter 2

Bobbie had driven a little Hyundai similar to the one she drove now once before, in Spain, and she recognised the way it seemed to hop about and the distinctive busy clattering engine note. It seemed this one was an earlier model and was obviously well used.

It rattled it's way to her destination well enough, however, as she pulled up outside Pauline Patrick's little cottage in good time for their appointment. And to the accompaniment of a small dog barking within, she rang the doorbell.

'I knew you had booked into the hotel. Is everything all right there?' Mrs Patrick said as she opened the door.

This rather unexpected opening line caught Bobbie off guard a little.

'Er, yes. Thank you … why did you …'

'Oh, sorry,' said Pauline as she ushered Bobbie into

the little sitting room. 'I suppose you would say it is taking a proprietorial interest … you see my husband used to own that hotel and left it to me when he passed away.'

Bobbie noticed that, despite her Irish sounding name, her host spoke with a slightly clipped Surrey accent.

'Have you lived here long, Mrs Patrick,' asked Bobbie.

'About a year, and call me Pauline, please. And accept my apologies for asking about the hotel, you must think me very strange. It's just that since I found that dead body I seem to be all at sixes and sevens somehow.'

'I imagine it was a considerable shock. What did you do when you came across it?'

'Well, the first thing was to try to get Buster here to leave it alone. The little rascal had slipped his collar and was pawing at it as I tried to get him back under control,' Pauline reached down and patted the little dog as she spoke. 'Would you like some tea?'

'No thank you, I had a coffee at the hotel, but don't let me stop you … So what did you do?'

'Well, I called the police and they told me to stay put, so I had to wait by the body until they arrived with the coastguard people. I can't say that was a pleasant experience and the body had obviously been in the water some time.'

'I'm told the hands and feet were tied together?'

'Yes, and behind the poor man's back, so that he was tied into a sort of kneeling position with his wrists and ankles tightly bound with thin blue nylon rope. You could see it was tight because it had cut into the flesh around the ankles where his trousers had ridden up a bit. There was no blood, of course. He had been in the water too long for that, although the body was not yet bloated, probably because the sea was quite cold.'

'Revolting, and an unpleasant experience for you having to wait with the body.'
'Funnily enough it didn't smell, so he can't have been dead that long, but it was not an experience I should like to repeat in a hurry.'

'I can well imagine. So when the police arrived what did you do?'

'Well it was only young Shaun and his Sergeant from the local station, and until the coastguard people got there I'm not sure they knew what to do. Shortly after that though, an ambulance arrived and a chap from the … the Irish Times, I think it was, turned up and started taking photographs. They seemed very professional, as if this sort of thing was commonplace for them.'

'The Irish Times, you say?'

'Yes, the reporter chap seemed take charge of the situation on the beach and gave me his card. I've got it here somewhere …'

As Pauline rifled through her little bag amongst the dog treats and neatly rolled up poo bags, Bobbie took a look around her.

The little room they were in was obviously newly furnished and in a modern style. The smart leather chair on which she sat had electronic controls to adjust it in all sorts of directions and, on the other side of the fireplace, which contained a contemporary artificial fire with white gel 'coals', another identical chair was positioned facing a matching sofa, on which Pauline perched.

'Here we are,' she said now, handing the card to Bobbie. 'He said to call if I needed to talk to him, although I can't think why I would.'

'Well it is very kind of you to agree to see me, Pauline, and I do realise that the press can be a bit intrusive.'

'Not at all, he was the only one I've seen apart from you, and he told me that it was only because he was here to play golf that he got involved at all.'

'Well, I confess I'm a bit surprised at that. It can't be everyday a body washes up on the beach with a bullet hole in the head …'

'Do you want to know what I think,' said Pauline. 'I think it might be something to do with the IRA and that is why they are leaving it alone. I haven't lived in Ireland very long, but I have noticed that people don't mention all that sort of thing, but the tensions are obviously still there, under the surface. I think most of the folks round here would like to forget all about it and move on, but there are a few …'

'I suppose you would notice that sort of thing, running a hotel, I mean …'

'Oh no, I never worked in the hotel and neither did Barry, my husband. Barry inherited it, you see, and I'd never actually been here until he died.'

'I'm sorry, I didn't mean to …'

'Not at all. It was all rather a shock to me when I found out about this place, to be honest. I worked in a provincial solicitor's office and Barry worked in insurance in the City of London, and I had no idea this place even existed until he died.'

'Then how did you come to live here?' Bobbie asked.

'When it all came out about Barry owning the hotel I was intrigued so I came over for a look, and I sort of fell in love with the place. Barry also left me a bit of money so I decided to retire from Oakshott Parslow, the solicitors where I worked, and moved here.'

'I'm sorry,' said Bobbie sitting up straight in her chair, 'Did you say Oakshott Parslow?'

'Yes. Why?'

'Well that *is* a coincidence. Before I decided on a career as an investigative journalist I went for an interview with a firm of solicitors called Oakshott Parslow and Partners, in their conveyancing department.'

'Good heavens! Who interviewed you? Mr Shotter? He used to be my boss!'

'No, it was a Spanish chap who was just there for a few days to help out; and a Mr Ledger, the manager, I think.'
'Well I never! What a small world! I was with that firm for almost sixteen years and you must have gone along there as I left!'

'Good gracious! It is indeed a small world,' said Bobbie.

-ooo0ooo-

David was smiling broadly, much to Rosy's relief, as she drew up in the car she had just bought.

'It does look all right, doesn't it,' he said as he opened the door.

'I don't normally stop for hitchhikers,' said Rosy, 'but I'll make an exception this once for a handsome chap like you, so long as you behave and keep your hands to yourself. Hop in and I'll take you for a spin!'

Chuckling, David climbed aboard and Rosy, having stalled and then re-started the car, drove off around the residential roads of Putney.

'It needs filling up with petrol because I think it is running on fumes at the moment, so we could go round to the Shell Garage. How do you fancy taking it down to Janet and Geoff's place on Sunday?'

'What about insurance and all that sort of thing?'

'All sorted, although it cost a bit more than we originally thought. Fortunately the two hundred I got off the price covered that though, so we are all ready to hit the road!'

'Well done, Rosy!'

'Thank you, kind sir. Now, if you would like to buckle up, keeping your arms and legs inside the vehicle at all times and remain seated until the car comes to a complete stop at the end of the ride, we can see what this baby can do!'

-oo0Ooo-

Bobbie quickly got the message that the man from the coastguard's office was trying to fob her off.

No, she was informed, she could not interview the officer who attended on the beach, and with a firm 'No comment' to each of her subsequent questions, she had to leave it at that.

Constable Shaun Murphy was much more forthcoming, and was obviously very taken indeed with Bobbie's long auburn hair, slim frame, huge green eyes and tip-tilted nose, and he positively gabbled when she started to talk to him.

'I'm not supposed to be talking to anyone about it,'

he informed her. 'But so long as you don't tell my sergeant where you got it, I'll tell you what I know.'

'Was it you who Henry from our news agency spoke to, Shaun?' asked Bobbie gently.

'Um, yes,' said the young Constable, blushing to his roots. 'You won't tell the sergeant though, will you … I didn't ought to have said a word.'

'Your secret is safe with me, Shaun,' said Bobbie, fixing him with a shy smile and looking demurely up at him from behind lowered eyelids. 'What time do you get off duty? Perhaps we could go and have a coffee or something and talk about it.'

Shaun was very young, had led a sheltered life in rural Ballybunion and had never encountered anything like Bobbie before. Now, feeling as if he had swallowed something very large and spiny and unable to decide what to do with his hands or which leg to stand on next, he croaked out an answer of sorts.

'OK,' he said, and blushed ever more deeply.

-ooOOoo-

Pedro had to admit, even if only to himself, that he was always rather unsettled when Bobbie had to go away for her work.

He knew it could not be avoided, and supported her as much as he could by helping her to pack, and making sure she had everything she needed before she left on one of her trips, but he did not look forward to these little excursions.

Lately the time they had to spend apart had increased as Bobbie needed to frequently travel by train to Scotland to see her aunt. Pedro had joined her on those trips when he was able, at weekends, and had noticed a marked deterioration in her aunt between visits. He knew the circumstances, and that the outcome was inevitable, but the pain it caused his Bobbie hurt him too.

This current trip she was undertaking to Ireland was even more worrying in that involved a dead body, and the victim had without doubt been murdered. Pedro would much rather his Bobbie did not mix with murderers, even though he knew there was nothing he could do to discourage her from her chosen path.

As he put the plate he had used for his modest supper in the sink however, he was lifted out of his reverie when his mobile phone rang and the screen lit up with his favourite picture of Bobbie walking along the beach.

He snatched up the instrument and answered the call in excitement.

'Pedro, you are such a sweetie,' said the familiar voice. 'Fancy you copying out that passage from one of my books and slipping it into my bag!'

'I sorry, Bobbie, I not make the words good myself. Is

too difficulty for me. But now I reading all these books you got, I finding the things I want say to you. I hoping is OK?'

'It is lovely of you, dear sweet Pedro. I know you don't like it when I have to go away, and I miss you just as much as you miss me, you know ...'

'Yays. Missing my Bobbie, but I brave face. I helping the Bobbie and the Caroline, if I can, all the time. I want to help, you a know.'

'Yes, I do know, Pedro, although I can't see how you can help me much on this particular case at the moment, except of course to promise me that you are eating properly and managing all right.'

'I just a finished the supper, Bobbie. Made the salad. Is most easy.'

'Ready prepared salad from the supermarket?'

'Yays, is furry nice. Also the frankfurters. Is easy, just a open the tin! Is no problem.'

'You had frankfurters from a tin with salad?'

'Yays. I mean, no. The Pedro he no eat from a the tin! Pedro he do the cook properly. Is easy peasy put in the microwave, on the plate, no trouble!'

'Oh well, it makes a change from take-away I suppose.'

'Yays. I'm a eating healthy these days!'

-ooOOoo-

'He was one of those who work on the ships, you see.'

Shaun had agreed to meet Bobbie at Pauline Patrick's cottage and Pauline, who liked Shaun, seemed happy to get involved.

'They never settle in one place for long, that sort. I don't actually think he had ever been to Ballybunion before ... before ...'

'Yes, I see,' said Bobbie. 'But his name appeared on the Police Database?'

'Yes,' said Shaun as Pauline handed round the chocolate digestives. 'He had a record. Just minor stuff really. Punch-ups in pubs mostly. That sort of thing.'

'Nothing involving the "troubles" or the IRA, was there?' asked Pauline.

Shaun looked uncomfortable. In her direct way Pauline had obviously touched a nerve.

'Not really, but well, there was this one thing ...'

'Go on,' said Bobbie encouragingly.

'Well, it was a long time ago. Did I mention that he was nearly sixty years old? Well, erm... when he was about twenty years old, he was a junior member of the crew of a small cargo ship that the French impounded. That ship ... the ship he worked on was ... well, everyone knows about that ship.'

'I don't,' said Bobbie.

'Neither do I,' added Pauline.

'Ah well, no. I suppose you might not, being English and all.'

'What ship was this, Shaun?'

'Well you have got to understand that this was all a long time ago and things here in Ireland were very different then …'

'More tea?' said Pauline.

'Back then, before I was born, there was a lot of unrest and people took to being supporters of certain groups, sometimes under pressure from their families or to keep in with their friends and all.'

'In the "troubles" you mean?'

'Well, this was the start of one of the worst periods of all that, I suppose …'

'What was so special about the ship Eoin O'Grady was working on?' asked Bobbie, although she was beginning to suspect that she already knew.

'Well, we don't like to talk about these things now,' Shaun was visibly uncomfortable. 'It was … well, it was running guns from Libya to Ireland. It's a bit of history people don't like to be reminded of now …'

'Was the ship called The Eksund, Shaun … the ship

that contained the biggest haul of guns, ammunition and explosives that the IRA had ever tried to import?'

'Er, yes.' said Shaun and sank deeper into the sofa with his tea.

'Good Heavens! However did you know that Bobbie?' asked Pauline.

'The Eksund incident was quite notorious and my … my sources have told me a little about it,' Bobbie turned the pages of her notebook. 'I made some notes from a press clipping about it when I was looking into this … yes, here we are …

"In October 1987, the skipper, Adrian Hopkins, and three other men were arrested when the French navy intercepted a small freighter called the Eksund off the coast of Brest. On board was an arsenal containing 150 tons of weapons and munitions which were being supplied to the IRA by Libya's Colonel Gadaffi.

There were 1,000 mortars, thousands of rounds of ammunition, 20 surface-to-air missiles, 430 grenades, anti-aircraft machine-guns and 120 RPG rocket launchers." read Bobbie.

'Apparently the skipper had also made four other deliveries of weapons before that, but this one was on a much bigger scale.'

'Blimey!' said Pauline.

'I think I had better be going,' said Shaun, 'Me Ma will be cooking the tea.'

-ooO0oo-

Chapter 3

'**I**'m not sure I'm going to get much more done by staying on here, Pedro, so I'll be home tomorrow, I think.'

'Is good. Let me know when you back ... I cook the supper for you!'

'You are going to cook supper for me, Pedro? How kind of you!'

'Yays. Got the rest of a the tin of the frankfurters use up. Maybe I make the pasta for to go with them?'

'Ah, well ... I'm not actually sure what time I'll be back, sweetie,' said Bobbie, revolted. 'And I wouldn't want your supper to ruin ... so might it be better to wait until I'm actually home, then we can order in pizza or something.'

'Oh, OK, my Bobbie ... I just a thinking! Can put the frankfurters on a the pizza! Be most nice!'

'I'll see you tomorrow, Pedro.'

-ooOOoo-

Bobbie called the cottage in Scotland to give her aunt an update, but ended up speaking to an answering machine, so she tried her mobile.

That also went to an answering machine, but a few minutes later her aunt returned the call.

'Its nothing, really. Just some bureaucratic mix-up, probably, but they want to keep me in for a couple more days to keep an eye on me. I feel fine, honestly.'

'You don't sound fine, auntie. I'll see if I can get a flight direct from here to Glasgow and come straight to the hospital …'

'You will do no such thing, Roberta,' said Caroline, with some of the old fire back in her increasingly husky voice. 'You will return to London and start to write up the story; and I'll look forward to your draft by email. Then, after your trip at the weekend to see Geoffrey and Janet, you can book a train ticket and stay in the cottage, where I want you to find some press clippings I have there that pertain to this case, so we can write up the back story together. Are we clear?'

'How did you know that we were planning to go to Geoff and Janet for Sunday lunch?'

'Ah-ha! A good journalist never reveals her sources, and my spies are everywhere!'

'No, really.'

'And also I had a chat with Geoffrey on the telephone and he told me you and Rosy and Pedro and ay, erm, David, isn't it … are all gathering there. Quite a little party. I'm only sorry I can't make it myself.'

'Oh Auntie Caroline. Are you really all right? I'm sure I could get up there easily enough if …'

'No Bobbie, there is nothing to be concerned about, really. Now let me tell you about these press clippings and where I have filed them in the cottage. There is so much mess and muddle in there, you will never be able to find them without a map and a couple of well trained Sherpas on your own!'

-oo0Ooo-

'So if you like, Bobbie, David and I could pick you up in our new car and run you down there on Sunday.'

'But wouldn't that be going out of your way, Rosy?'

'Only the tiniest little detour is required, and if anything goes wrong, there will be more of us to push!'

'You don't seem very confident in it …'

'Just joshing. Actually it seems pretty robust. I've just been out with a bucket of steaming soapy water and the Marigolds and given it a jolly good going over inside. Now that the top crust of the grime of the ages has been removed, the no doubt fossilised remains beneath do seem quite solid. All in all, I'm rather pleased with it.'

'I look forward to seeing it ...'

'Well, by the time you do, you might need sunglasses because David has promised to pick up some polish and what-not on his way home and spend Saturday buffing the old paint up to a shine you can see your face in.'

Rosy drew a deep breath.

'Seriously though, don't get your hopes up too high. It is no limousine and is rather showing it's age. But it will do to get us mobile, and given that David can park near his office, it will save him having to slug it out on the underground trains each day.'

'How is it going in the new house?'

'Apartment, actually. It is a pity you couldn't come with us when we went to view it with that odious little agent. I would have appreciated your opinion. Not that we had much choice, mind. These rented places up here in the smoke do get snapped up with unseemly haste, and if we hadn't grabbed it when we did ...'

'You are not disappointed though, are you, Rosy?'

'Well, no. Not really. One would have preferred something with a little more elbow room, and perhaps a couple of roads over where the glitterati live, but needs must.'

'Are you allowed to decorate it and so-on?'

'My dear child, not to decorate it would be a crime. The huge red roses on a blue and white background on one wall in the lounge give David nightmares, and the luminous bright yellow on the kitchen walls is rather too sudden in the early morning, especially if we have been revelling the night before.'

'Oh dear.'

'But have no fear. David has already stripped the wallpaper off in the hall, and once the plasterer has been to repair the damage, we are ready with a full set of paintbrushes to make the place liveable and draw out it's hidden Victorian charms. Now, what time shall we pick you up on Sunday?'

-oo0Ooo-

'To be honest, I was quite surprised to get a call from her,' said Geoff. 'Whilst I like and admire her, I can't say we have ever been close.'

'Well she is just tying up the loose ends, I suppose. It must be awful to know that your life is coming to an end.'

'She actually mentioned that, Janet, and she said she was grateful to have a bit of time to tidy things up, and say things she should have said before and all that sort of thing. It is what this is doing to Bobbie that worries me.'

'What did she say then?'

'She wanted to tell me that ... it is not easy to explain ... she wanted to say that she knows how close I am to Bobbie and how I'm like a father to her, sort of. She wanted me to tell Bobbie how much I love her, and made me promise that I would.'

Janet reached for a tissue from the box on the table.

'Then she told me that she is leaving everything to her. Her cottage, all her money, everything.'

'She is not that well off, is she?'

'Well, I'm not so sure, that is why it was such a surprise. She told me that her solicitor ... I've written his name down on the pad ...would be in touch when it ... when she ... Anyway, she told me some of what to expect.'

'I don't understand?'

'She is leaving Bobbie her business, and that might not be as straight-forward as it seems. We knew she had been involved in all sorts of dangerous things when she was younger, but there are legacies from that.
She has helped all kinds of people that she met throughout her life. I had no idea about this, Janet, but she supports a charity that she actually set up herself which looks after distressed and retired journalists.

She said the details would all be handed over when she ... when she ...' Geoff coughed, caught his breath and continued, 'Handed over by the solicitor and she wants me to take on the role of trustee to help Bobbie manage it.'

'Oh Geoff. Do you know what this is all about?'

'No, and although I tried to ask, she got very short of breath, and I wanted to let her talk, rather than interrupting her. I thought I would ask Bobbie what she knows about it, or get her to ask Caroline for some more detail. I'm a bit nervous about this, I have to confess, and I don't think Caroline is going to be with us for long now.'

'Bobbie's going to be heartbroken.'

'I'm afraid so. We must be prepared to do what we can to support her.'

-ooo0ooo-

Saturday morning dawned bright and clear and Pedro, ever attentive, bought Bobbie tea in bed.

Oh, thank you, sweetie!' she said, accepting the hot mug he handed her. 'It is so nice to be able to wake up in my own bed with a cup of tea.'

'Yays. Is same for me too, though I not liking the tea. Only liking the wake up with the Bobbie. I just a come back in for minute...'

'Mind you don't spill my tea,' said Bobbie, placing the mug on her bedside table. 'Stop wriggling Pedro ... Pedro ... what are you doing?'

'Oh Bobbie, I'm loving the Saturday morning got the no work ... I'm loving you too Bobbie ...'

-ooO0oo-

The Irish Times published a very short item about the body on Ballybunion beach on page three and having stated that the police were looking into the circumstances around the death, left it at that.

The news feed Caroline kept running on her mobile phone had a 'search' facility and it took her some time to find even that small mention of the incident. Perhaps, she thought, Pauline Patrick was right and the full significance of the discovery of the body was being suppressed.
But, if Bobbie had found the information she needed, that was about to change.

Although the nurses at the hospital had frowned at the idea, Caroline had set up an efficient and effective 'workstation' on the tilting table which fitted over her hospital bed.

Using a mobile 'MiFi' device to avoid paying the hospital for using their WiFi, her powerful laptop took pride of place next to her two mobile phones, a large pad of paper and several pens.

On the foot of the bed lay several daily papers which she had arranged to have delivered each morning, and she had positioned the individual hospital television, on its flexible bracket, so that she could see it easily.

The nurses had not, so far, noticed the small device which she had plugged into the back of the television which functioned to override the restricted hospital tuning and allowed her to access a range of local and foreign news channels or use the screen as a second monitor for her laptop at the touch of a button.

By pressing just one key on her laptop, Caroline could conceal what she was really watching and return the TV to the jaunty 'Breakfast Show' considered suitable for the patients by the hospital authorities.

The visits from the various nurses and doctors were infrequent, but Caroline didn't have time to be bored.

-ooO0oo-

Pauline Patrick had become very fond of young Constable Shaun Murphy and today she invited him to stop for a cup of tea when he passed by, as she was tidying the hedge in her front garden.

He seemed very young and vulnerable, and to Pauline at least, not really fitted for the hurly burly of life as a policeman. She thought that she would like to encourage him, but that he needed some help if he was going to progress in his chosen career.
If, she felt, he could develop the quick and incisive

brain of someone like Bobbie Bassington, who had greatly impressed her, he might do well, but he would need some coaching to learn how to look for the next step when trying to unravel a mystery.

Perhaps, she thought, Bobbie might be prepared to help him.

As they passed the time of day and the tea slowly cooled, they inevitably fell to taking about the body on the beach.

Shaun felt comfortable with Pauline, which was an unusual state of affairs for him. He frequently felt out of his depth at the police station as he tried to learn the finer points of his new vocation, and it was nice to have someone to talk to that he felt would be supportive. At least she might not be critical like his sergeant, back at the station, who was quite likely to laugh at him and tease when he made a mistake or did not understand something.

Pauline asked him if he knew which ship Eoin O'Grady had been working on and if it was Irish owned, and Shaun explained that they found a payslip in his pocket which showed he had just finished a trip with his last employer, 'Colin Patterson Seafrieght' who managed a handful of container ships running between various ports in northern Europe or the west of Ireland, across the Atlantic.

He explained that the police had contacted the company and been told which ship he worked on last, but they had not yet received much other information.

Whilst the company's personnel record keeping seemed a little haphazard they had at least established that Eoin O'Grady had not worked for them for very long and may have been on his first ship for the company.

As Shaun finished his tea and passed on his way, Pauline fought with her conscience. After looking at the thing from all angles, she decided that Shaun's information might help to catch a killer, and Bobbie Bassington was much more likely to spot how it could help than poor inexperienced little Shaun, so she made a call on her mobile and left her a message.

-ooOOoo-

'They are here,' called Geoff, looking out of the front window.

'Right-ho,' Janet replied from the kitchen.

'Hello there,' said Geoff, opening the front door.

David was unwinding himself from the driver's seat as Geoff approached, and the other occupants of the car were opening doors and climbing out.

'Hello Uncle Geoff,' said Bobbie, 'Here we all are.'

'Just about,' scowled Rosy. 'We got stopped by the Police just outside Guildford.'

'It hardly delayed us at all, Rosy,' said David.

'Thanks to your breakneck driving,' added Rosy.

'Oh dear, did you get stopped for speeding?' asked Geoff.

'No, it was just some nonsense about the car not being taxed, but when they checked again on their radio, they found that it was all legal and correct … it was just that the database had not updated since we picked the car up.'

'Is exciting. The police he put on the siren and the lights a flashing. Like the police chase in a film, only we no run away,' added Pedro helpfully.

'Oh well, no harm done, and you are not in the least bit late,' Geoff held open the front door and ushered them inside. 'The car looks pretty good though, perhaps we can have a proper look at it later.'

'Mmm! Lunch smells wonderful!' said Bobbie, skipping to the kitchen to embrace Janet.

-oo0Ooo-

Chapter 4

Life as crew on a container ship crossing the Atlantic is not for the faint hearted.

Bobbie looked up 'life on-board a container ship' and found several magazine articles from people who had direct experience of it.

She read that there are clear, almost colonial, dividing lines between the crew members, with the upper echelon of engineers and the captain usually being white Europeans, whilst the other seamen are most commonly Filipinos who work on contracts typically lasting nine months of the year, often without leaving the boat at all, even in port.

The reports went on to describe how the more senior crew tend to have four month contracts, and sleep in separate and slightly better, although hardly luxurious, accommodation on board. The two groups eat in separate 'messes' and do not socialise much, keeping mostly within their own ethnic groups. But there are no days off on cargo ships and the crews work continually, so there is not much time for leisure anyway.

The work, she read, is hard and physical and there is always something to do on ships which are at sea the best part of 365 days of the year, often in atrocious weather conditions and needing constant repair and maintenance. Time is very definitely money on these huge vessels and their owners do not allow work to stop, ever.

Any time spent in port, one article stated, cost the owners money and there are strict protocols for loading and unloading the ships as quickly as possible, using the brief time when the engines are idle to carry out repairs and maintenance, and take on huge quantities of fuel.

She was surprised to learn that there are over 50,000 container ships worldwide, and even the smaller ones can burn fifty tons of crude, the dirtiest fuel there is, every twenty-four hours.

There is typically no doctor or medical staff amongst the crew on a container ship, and the magazine stated that those on board usually have no idea what is in any of the containers, except those needing temperature control, which they monitor, or if there is anything dangerous, which has to be declared. Otherwise there could be anything in the boxes from soya beans to motorcars, and from cheap umbrellas to canned tuna.

Eoin O'Grady had been working as Second Engineer on a ship shuttling across the Atlantic the 4,028 nautical miles between Philadelphia and Antwerpen, called Galway Enterprise. The name made it sound more like a cross between a fishing boat and a spaceship than a battered old container ship, but the money on offer on these boats is good for those that can tolerate the work, and the owners keep producing cargos to be shipped, so as an itinerant, but experienced sailor, Eoin was presumably happy enough to join the company.

It was by no means the first job he had on the container ships and his whole career had been spent at sea in one form or another.

Although once married, very briefly, he had no family except a brother who lived in Dublin and worked as a bus driver.

With only this limited information to hand, Bobbie was going to find background checks into his life hard to do.

-ooo0oo-

'Ford spent a fortune developing this car, David, and it was, and still is, very successful. I don't think you will regret buying one of these.'

Full of roast pork, and at that comfortable point in digesting a substantial Sunday lunch when the conversation becomes muted and the plates are cleared away, Geoff and David had gone outside to look at the car.

'It was Rosy's idea to buy a car, actually,' said David. 'I wasn't really sure that we needed one, but she seemed determined that our parking space needed to be filled.'

'I thought it might be her idea.'

'Oh, don't misunderstand me. I think it will be jolly useful, but when Rosy gets an idea into her head ...'

'You mean she is determined?'

'She bought it on a whim, really. We hadn't actually been looking for a car, well, not really, but Rosy has what I've heard described as a "whim of iron" sometimes.'

Geoff chuckled as he added that he knew precisely what he meant.

'And of course she is the sweetest girl you could hope to meet most of the time, but she does like to get her own way, and being on the substantial side, can deliver quite a convincing shove when thwarted.' David looked wistful. 'We were taking a walk down the towpath by the Thames when she first mentioned the idea, and when I demurred I was lucky to be able to stay on my feet and not end up in the water!'

'What are you two giggling about,' asked Janet, joining them on the driveway.

-oo0Ooo-

"Hackdoone House" had a different name when, in 1990, Caroline Bassington purchased the derelict timber and asbestos bungalow on a former smallholding in the hills above Dorking in an auction. It took her the next three years to convince the Local Council to give planning permission to redevelop it into what is was now.

Housing forty two elderly and disabled persons, when fully occupied, the two large linked single storey buildings now on the site stood a little further away from the road than the original bungalow, and were protected from it by a long curved driveway with substantial gates set in a brick arch at the entrance.

Of the permanent residents, twelve had spent their careers in journalism in one form or another, and eight of those were quite severely disabled.

John Parish was the most vocal of this set, despite having lost both legs and suffered serious injuries in an explosion while reporting as a freelancer in Northern Ireland. He was the inspiration, at least in part, for the establishment of this little community.

He served now as one of three trustees who managed the small charity, set up to provide help and housing to injured or distressed journalists in need of support. There was no shortage of applicants from the ranks of the usually freelance front-line media people the charity sought to help, but funding was always a limiting factor.

A balance had been found when all but twelve of the rooms providing nursing care were let to private residents, and the cross-subsidy the commercial operation generated paid for the care of those who could not pay for themselves. It worked well when all the rooms were let, but as inevitably there were regularly voids as new residents were sought to replace those who passed away, there were moments in the past when the administrators of the facility held their breaths and finances were balanced on a knife edge.

The unfortunate truth was that freelancing journalists are often too wrapped up in their work to plan adequately for their retirement or, given the precarious nature of their profession, often lacked the time or money to make provision, by way of insurance, to cover eventualities such as accidents, which may disrupt their income. Many were butterflies who lived in the moment, and whether seeking adventure or pursuing the next story, they were not good at planning ahead.

John Parish, although dependant on the Charity, did his best to support the home with his own fund-raising efforts, and he grew a range of vegetables, apples and soft fruit in the fertile soil around the buildings. These he sold either at the gate or more consistently to local restaurants who liked the idea of limiting the distance their ingredients had to travel to reach the plate. Considering the extent of his disabilities, his efforts were remarkable, and the operation now employed a young part-time horticultural trainee with support from the local college, and found volunteers among several of the residents who were interested in, and capable of, working the land.

They made jams in the kitchen using the fruit, and cider from the apples in a substantial but very elderly shed in the orchard. Oddly though, although the apple crop was usually quite reliable, very little cider actually got to leave the facility.

"Hackdoone House" had been incorporated as a limited company on the advice of the solicitor who, with Caroline, made up the remainder of the Board of Trustees, and although initially set up with Caroline's donation, the facility now had a mortgage which paid for the construction of ten new rooms, the provision of a small swimming/therapy pool, various state of the art assisted bathing pieces of equipment and a secondhand minibus for excursions. The two trustees knew that Caroline's Will provided for another very generous legacy which would pay this loan off and set the facility on a firm and solid financial footing for many years to come, but Caroline had insisted that nobody else should be told, so that the staff continued to diligently and economically manage the business for the benefit of the residents, and did not become complacent.

It was, she felt, a sound and prudent strategy, and Caroline, leaning back on her pillows, had just finished typing it into a document to be given to the new Trustee, on appointment, when the time came.

-oo0Ooo-

'But this is the first I have heard of this, Uncle Geoff. I had no idea that Auntie Caroline wanted you to be a Trustee of anything, let alone that she was involved in a charity.'

'Well, that is what she asked me to do. And not just any charity, one she actually set up herself.'

'It seems there is quite a lot about Auntie Caroline's past that we don't know,' said Bobbie, and as the tears filled her eyes she added, 'And I don't think we have long left to find out.'

Geoff had asked Bobbie to take a stroll around the garden with him before she went home after their Sunday lunch, and what he had to say had surprised her.

'I'm going up to Scotland tomorrow so I'll ask her to explain, of course, but from what you said she might just say wait until the solicitor reads the Will. I'm not sure if she will tell me anything more about it.'

'I realise that, Bobbie. But if you can't get any information, don't upset her, especially as she is currently in hospital.'

'Oh, Uncle Geoff. I've got a horrible feeling that she is not coming out again this time. She puts a brave face on it and never complains, but she is becoming so frightfully thin and seems to have shrunk.'

'I know. She got very breathless when she called me, and I had to wait for her to be able to continue several times.' Geoff looked at his feet. 'Look Bobbie, when the inevitable happens, why don't you and Pedro come and stay down here for a few days? Janet and I want to take care of you, while you get over it. And … and … I love you very much you know.'

Bobbie collapsed into his arms and wept.

Chapter 5

The six hour train journey to Glasgow, starting very early and catching the first train at three minutes past four on a wet Monday morning, was not something Bobbie had been looking forward to, and this time there were several delays along the way.

But by the time she had changed trains for the last stretch of the journey to Milngavie and then been taken by taxi to Killearn and Caroline's pretty cottage, the sun was out and Bobbie's gloomy mood had lifted somewhat.

She had decided to dump her overnight bag at the cottage, find the newspaper cuttings her aunt had requested and go straight on to the hospital to see her, and pausing only to make a cup of refreshing tea when she arrived, she was about to put her plan into action when her phone rang in her pocket.

'Hello there Bobbie! How the devil are you,' Rosy's

bluff manner was made all the more noticeable when using the telephone.

'Better before you started bawling down the phone at me, Rosy. And how are you.'

'Splendid, splendid, splendid, splendid, thank you. And all the better for talking to you, my bonhomous bright and bounding Bassington.'

'And nice to hear from you, too,' chortled Bobbie. 'Was there anything, or did you just want to exercise your lungs with a bit of shouting?'

'No, important mission actually. Got the post when I got home last night, and there was a rather jolly invitation to join a weekend party in it from your old school pal, Toenail, or the recently elevated Countess of Wymondham if you prefer. I assume you got one too, but I'm aware you are up in Scotland, so won't have seen it, so thought I'd give you a ring with the news.'

'Toenail? A weekend party? Well, she did say she was planning something pretty spectacular when she got a bit more settled. When is it?'

'Jolly decent of her to invite David and I too, I thought. Particularly as we have only met her a couple of times, after you introduced us. It is in a couple of months time and is in Norfolk, of all places.'

At about the time Tonya became The Countess of Wymondham, having recently made an excellent marriage, Bobbie had introduced her old friend to her Aunt Caroline and smiled at the memory of the conversation.

'This is my old school friend, Toenail, Auntie Caroline. Or rather I should say this is Tonya Ophelia Naill, known to all at the dear old school as Toenail, due to the rough work perpetrated at her baptism which left her with the unfortunate name T. O. Naill embroidered on her school gym bag.'

Rosy had more to say on the matter and assailed Bobbie's eardrum once again.

'Thought I'd give you a ring to offer transport, assuming you are going. Splitting the petrol cost four ways will be a help, and jolly 'green', wouldn't you say? And also Norfolk is a mysterious place to David and I, so if the natives don't prove friendly, at least we will go to our doom in good company.'

'That is very kind of you, Rosy, and a good idea. Presumably this means you are becoming more confident in the abilities of your new car?'

'Oh yes, no problem there. It may be quite old but I think it keeps on running by force of habit, so it should be fine.'

'So what does the invitation say?'

'I have it here ... "The Earl and Countess of Wymondham will be at home and request the pleasure of your company for a celebration of summer." Then there is the date and so on and then

"We hope you can join us for the weekend and we would be pleased to offer accommodation on the Friday and Saturday nights within Belcher Court for the event." All sounds rather good, don't you think?'

'Smashing!' said Bobbie. 'Good old Toenail. That really is something to look forward to.'

-ooO0oo-

'That actually went quite well.' Geoff and Janet were reviewing the conversation in the garden when Geoff told Bobbie about "Hackdoone House".

'Well, that depends on how you look at it, Geoff. I saw her crying on your shoulder through the kitchen window.'

'It breaks my heart to see her like that, but I'm afraid there might be quite a bit more of that when Caroline passes away.'

'You two are so close ...'

'Yes, and by the way I did ask her if she wanted to come and stay with us for a while when it happens, although I didn't get an answer. And ... and as Caroline asked ... I did tell her that I loved her.'

'Good. At least she knows we are prepared to help her when she needs us, although I rather suspect she will also involve you in the arrangements and sorting out her house and so on up in Scotland,'

'Yes, we must be prepared for that too. By the way, speaking of Scotland, I saw Duncan-Browne in the bakers the other day, and he thinks we could organise another salmon fishing trip up there soon.'

'The bakers? What were you doing in there, Geoffrey? Not doughnuts again?'

-ooOOoo-

On his way home on Monday, Pedro remembered his promise to Bobbie to eat properly and healthily, and called into the small 'Tesco' by the station to pick up supplies.

He was hungry, and made the more-so when he saw the appetising looking steaks in their plastic packages on the shelves. Remembering that meat seems to shrink when you cook it, he chose a 480 gram rump steak and put it in his basket.
It would go well, he was thinking, with the 'oven chips' he was about to add, when he remembered Bobbie's assertion that chips were not healthy.

Looking around him he saw tins of spaghetti ... Pasta, he thought. Bobbie would approve of that, and so the can of Heinz spaghetti in tomato sauce joined the steak in the shopping basket.

Satisfied that he had a supper for tonight that Bobbie would approve of, he was all set, and he headed for the check-out.

-ooOOoo-

In Caroline's cottage, in an upstairs room, there were stacks of dusty black metal storage containers of the type used by banks as safe deposit boxes. They lined almost the whole of one wall and each had a drawer with a metal slot of the sort you find on filing cabinets to take a label, and a keyhole, although, as far as she could see, none had keys. Some had yellowing and faded labels in place, some did not. But Bobbie had been directed to the second row on the right, when Caroline had told her where to look for the newspaper clippings about Eoin O'Grady's ship.

Starting at the bottom of the row Bobbie drew open the first drawer. It stuck and was awkward to access, and as she pulled at it and tried to open it, the whole stack above it slid forward slightly and for a moment she thought it might topple over onto her.

That first drawer was completely full of sheets of paper, including old bank statements and similar, no doubt once important communications. She struggled to close the complaining, squeaking, metal drawer and moved on to the one above it.

The stack wobbled ominously again as she pulled at the little handle of the second drawer, but this time, apart from a dead moth, the drawer was empty.

The stack was six boxes high, and Bobbie decided that it might be wise to take the topmost boxes off the stack before she tried to open any more, to avoid causing an avalanche, if the unstable pile did collapse. Fortunately the top drawer was quite light, and sliding it onto the carpet, she opened it to find it contained several photographs and a handful of old-fashioned cine-film canisters. Not what she was looking for.

She was taking the next, slightly heavier, box down from the stack and preparing to position it on the floor, ready to open it, when she noticed that moving it had revealed another set of smaller cardboard shoe boxes, stacked up behind the the metal containers, in what appeared to be the otherwise concealed opening of a small former fireplace set into the wall.

None of these smaller boxes had the filing cabinet style label holders although one, halfway down, had a handwritten sticker on the front with the name 'Nicola' in a clumsily drawn heart on one corner.

This box was much more battered than the others, and although it was not what she was supposed to be looking for, it was so unlike the rest of the much more businesslike boxes, that Bobbie was intrigued and she reached forward to draw it out.

It did occur to her that this box might contain something her aunt would regard as private as she lifted the lid, but it was too late now, and Bobbie was too fascinated to learn what it contained to stop herself.

Inside, half the box contained a small stack of

letters in envelopes addressed to her aunt in neat handwriting, and to the back there was something else under some yellowing tissue-paper.

Bobbie gingerly lifted the crumpled paper out of the box and then gasped as she revealed a small handmade teddy bear and a pair of tiny white knitted booties, obviously meant for a new-born baby.

Under those was a neatly folded birth certificate, and there was a death certificate underneath that. Both documents bore the same date. Nicola Ann had only lived for one day.

Moving the tiny booties to one side, Bobbie read the mother's name on the birth certificate and noticed that the little stack of three or four letters was propped up by a rather ostentatiously presented invitation to the 'Annual Officer's Ball' in her aunt's name. On one corner was written 'Guest of Captain C. Duncan-Browne'.

Bobbie read the invitation again, as the realisation of what this sad little box represented washed over her.

-ooo0ooo-

Chapter 6

On reaching the hospital, Bobbie enquired as to her aunt's whereabouts and was directed to a little side ward on the first floor.

The ward was divided into separate rooms with partly glazed doors off a central corridor, and each door had a set of holders for files and clipboards attached either on the door or on the wall outside. Bobbie knew that the clipboard to the right was where the nurses regularly recorded blood pressure, temperature and so on, but she was alarmed to see a triangular sticker on the right hand corner of the front page of the papers with the letters 'DNR' in red letters. Bobbie knew enough about the code doctors and nurses used to know that DNR meant 'Do Not Resuscitate'.

Having paused to collect herself after that shock, she took a deep breath and pushed open the door to her aunt's room.

Another shock awaited her as she approached the bed. Her aunt had tubes going to her nose connected to a machine beside the bed and an oxygen cylinder.

Caroline was asleep, propped up on her pillows with her mouth open and gently snoring. She seemed very small and her skin had a slightly grey tinge.

Bobbie noticed the TV monitor over the bed seemed to be showing some French television news show with the sound muted, and the laptop in front of her on her makeshift 'workstation' had gone into sleep mode due to lack of use.

The pad next to the laptop had a series of notes in a quite shaky hand that was not at all like the firm, bold style her aunt usually adopted in her notebooks. Bobbie also noticed that she still had a pen in her hand. That hand was bandaged and she could see that a 'cannula' had been inserted with a tube which was connected to the machine.

That machine now made a series of clicks and a beep which woke Caroline with a start.

'Good Lord,' she whispered. 'How long have you been here?'

'Just arrived, Auntie Caroline, how are you feeling?'

'I jolly sight better than I no doubt look, Bobbie. They do make such a fuss, and this ruddy thing in the back of my hand makes it painful to write or brush my hair

…'

'Would you like me to brush your hair, auntie?' Bobbie looked around for a hairbrush.

'Would you mind? Nobody could call me vain, but I do feel somewhat disheveled and not very presentable with uncombed hair.'

-ooOOoo-

'And how did you get on with parking it at work, David?'

Rosy was interested to hear how David coped with his drive to work, and having heard him complain about the cyclists and the traffic, although he left far too early to catch the worst of it, just in case, now she was interested in whether the promised easy parking at his office materialised.

'No problem at all, Rosy. Although I was at work much too early so the car park was almost empty. My line manager, Simon, says he will sign off the form for me to be allowed to use a parking space in the underground bit, so it is going to be even better.'

'Underground parking? So it won't be out in the weather, you mean?'

'Yes, although it is on a first come first served basis, and if the big bosses are in or there are important visitors, sometimes areas of it are cordoned off for their use, so you do have to take pot luck.'

'Wow. How important do you have to be as a visitor to get a designated parking space in the underground garage when you want to pop in and cash a cheque or something?'

'Er, no, Rosy. It is not that sort of bank. It is the corporate HQ and there isn't a banking hall as such. The nearest straightforward branch is a hundred yards down the road. The bit that was a normal bank on the ground floor once is now the staff gym, and some executive dining rooms the Directors use to entertain important customers, as I understand it.'

'Well even so, parking in the posh bit of Central London is one helluva perk to go with your job, isn't it!'

'Yes, I'm very lucky.'

'And so am I, David. You might be a great lumbering clumsy clot most of the time, but I am impressed with your exciting career prospects. How long before they invite you to join the Board and give you your own office with an en-suite swimming pool or something?'

-ooO0oo-

'So your draft layout of the story was fine and now that we have gone through the press cuttings I asked you to find, can I leave it to you to incorporate that information and draw up the final report.'

'What, me? Write it up finally, I mean. Do think I could

...'

'Certainly you can do that, Bobbie. I have complete confidence in you, and you need to start doing this on your own. Show me the finished text, if you like, but honestly I am sure you will make a great job of it without me breathing down your neck all the time.'

Bobbie's subconscious mind picked up and focussed on the words "leave it to you", "start doing this on your own" and "without me breathing down your neck", and all of that reminded her of Caroline's terminal diagnosis and how little time she had left. She pulled herself together with an effort and thanked her aunt for her confidence in her.

'Um,' she said now. 'Uncle Geoff has told me about your phone call and Hackdoone House ...'

'I didn't think Geoffrey would be able to keep his mouth shut. I was hoping not to have to get into all that.'

'I'm sorry, but he was quite concerned about it all ...'

'Yes well, in the interests of planning ahead I had anticipated that this might happen, so I have put together a sort of guide to how Hackdoone House works and what is involved in running it. I've emailed it to Max Sewell, my solicitor, who you met if you recall.' Caroline had to pause to catch her breath after that little speech, but when she recovered she added, 'So in the light of events I will forward the email to you and you can read it and print a copy off for Geoffrey.'

'Thank you, auntie. It sounds a fantastic thing to have done ...'

'Do you mind if we move on from that now, Bobbie. They will be round with supper in a moment and I don't want to inflict having to watch them trying to force that foul muck down me on you, and you must be tired after your journey. Can you come and see me again in the morning?'

'I'm sorry, you are tired. I hope I haven't worn you out.'

'Not at all, but watching the staff shovelling food into us sickly old fossils is not anything that should be imposed on a lovely young girl in the prime of life. Time enough for that in years to come!'

Bobbie laughed and offered to help, which Caroline dismissed with a wave of her good hand.

'No chance,' she said. 'Now I can hear the squeaky wheeled trolley of doom down the end of the corridor, so if there is nothing else ... I understand visiting starts at ten o-clock in the morning. If you work on the Eoin O'Grady text this evening and get it finished, perhaps we could go through it tomorrow.'

-oo0Ooo-

Pauline was surprised to get a text message from Bobbie Bassington, but quietly pleased that she was still prepared to involve her in what she was doing.

It wasn't much of a favour to ask, as she saw Shaun

most mornings when he walked past the cottage, and usually passed the time of day with him.

It was quite straightforward to ask Shaun if the police knew what Eoin O'Grady was doing for work when he was shot, given that the payslip in his pocket showed that his contract with the container ship, Galway Enterprise, had recently ended.

Shaun saw no reason not to tell Pauline and, over a mug of hot tea and a chocolate digestive, told her that the Dublin police had interviewed Eoin O'Grady's brother who thought that, between container ship contracts, he was occasionally skippering a charter boat doing deep water fishing trips out of the village of Kilbaha just up the coast.

He explained that the sergeant was asked to look into which boat he was working on but had not got far with it yet and would have to get round to visiting the little police house near Kilbaha soon to find out more from the local Constable based there.

The sergeant, he explained had not attached much importance to the matter because, as he said, Eoin O'Grady was dead, wasn't he, so wasn't going anywhere. There had been two car thefts in the meantime which were number one on their list, not least because one of the cars belonged to the Mayor's wife.

-ooO0oo-

Bobbie made herself supper and put in a call to Pedro

before she settled down to work on the article.

Pedro had proudly told her that he had cooked himself a healthy supper and there was enough left over for lunch tomorrow, although he had decided he preferred longer pieces of spaghetti and didn't like the tomato sauce.

After the third attempt to get him to explain what he meant, she gave up and said he could tell her all about it when she got home.

She saw that the email from Caroline had arrived, and she thought of calling her uncle Geoff and explaining about the document Caroline had prepared for them about Hackdoone House, but decided to do it in the morning and to dedicate herself for the rest of the evening to putting together the story of Eoin O'Grady's life in a readable and interesting form.

The ending, if their investigations had to stop now, was rather inconclusive and unsatisfactory but, she thought, it would have to do. For now she had to work with what she had got.

-ooo0oo-

Chapter 7

Bobbie was at the hospital in good time on Tuesday morning and she had to wait to be admitted when visiting time started. She knew that she had to catch the afternoon train back to London because she had to attend her college on Wednesday, and for the rest of the week.

She also knew that she had to submit a series of essays which she had not finished, or at least tidied up enough to be presentable. So, having spent the evening putting the final touches to the Eoin O'Grady article, she had decided to use the time on the train today to get the college work done.

Her course would soon be coming to a close and she would at last be free of college commitments, but with her Auntie Caroline being quite so unwell, she wished she did not have to return to London and could stay by her side.

Only her aunt's insistence that the college course came first maintained her resolve however, and she was very concerned that her aunt's condition would get worse while she was away.

She was startled out of her reverie by her phone ringing in her pocket, and surprised to see that the caller was Pauline Patrick from Ballybunion.

'There has been a development,' Pauline said. 'I've just seen Constable Shaun and he told me that the Coastguard have discovered a partly burnt out fishing boat abandoned at sea and drifting about five miles off the coast of Kilbaha. It is the boat Eoin O'Grady had been working on, between contracts on container ships, apparently.'

'Wow. Thank you, Pauline, that might be just the break we have been needing on this case. What more do you know?'

'Shaun said there is just a local visiting Constable in Kilbaha, which is a small fishing village up the coast from here, but he confirmed that O'Grady did work on a boat there sometimes, although he was not there much. The boat is one of a couple that do deep sea fishing charters for visitors. The coastguard are towing it back there, I think.'

'I ought to be there to take a look at it,' said Bobbie, but I'm up in Glasgow ... my aunt is in hospital here, you see ...'

'I thought you might say that you needed to see it,' Pauline paused as a thought formed in her mind. 'Look, I've got an idea. You are too far away to get here in time to see the boat before the police no doubt take it off somewhere to be examined … but nobody notices a little old lady walking a dog, so how about I drive up there and take Buster for a walk along by the harbour and see if I can get some pictures with my mobile phone?'

-ooOOoo-

Janet was interested to see that Bobbie had sent an email to her with an attachment.

'Sorry to bother you, Janet,' the message read. 'I know there is no point sending this to Uncle Geoff who won't know what to do with it and, if past form is anything to go by, will probably delete it or forward it to the Prime Minister or something, by accident.
This is the document my Aunt prepared to tell us what Hackdoone House is all about and what is involved in running it. She originally prepared this for her solicitor to pass on to us, but I managed to get her to show it to us now, which should ease Uncle Geoff's concerns.
Would you mind printing off a couple of copies and giving one to him?
Hope to see you soon, and thanks again for that wonderful lunch on Sunday.'

She did as she was asked and sat now with a coffee

reading the document through with Geoff.

'Well it seems straightforward enough,' she said. 'Obviously we haven't got the accounts yet, but Caroline says that it is financially sound and that it will shortly be debt free. What do you make of that?'

'Not a clue. Caroline has been secretive about this place until now, so who knows what disasters are waiting to be uncovered.'

'I don't think that is very fair, Geoff. Caroline has clearly invested a lot of money in this, and it says here it is run on a "not for profit" basis and breaks even each year.'

'I don't know enough about what "not for profit" means, Janet, but to me it might mean it doesn't make a profit and is going bust.'

'Caroline says the accounts have been professionally audited and that the profits are used to pay for the twelve retired or distressed ex-journalists who live there and that the charity is set up to support.'

'If there is a profit. Supposing there isn't … who is going to pay to support these people then? I'm worried that the burden of that might fall on the Trustees … and she wants me to be one of them!'

'We will have to ask Bobbie to use her investigative skills to find out, Geoff, and for now that can wait. Want to share the last of those doughnuts you have hidden in back of the cupboard with me?'

-ooO0Ooo-

Having gone through Bobbie's work with her and made a couple of minor suggestions, mostly to take out superfluous detail and to point out two or three spelling errors, Caroline relaxed back on her pillows.

Bobbie had almost decided to wait for another occasion, but realised, as her aunt struggled for breath, that it would be better to mention it now.

'Auntie. I don't want to upset you and I'm sorry, but when I found the newspaper cuttings, I also found this.' She drew the little hand made teddy bear from her bag and Caroline gasped as she gave it to her.

'Its none of my business, of course, but I imagine the cinema bombing in Dublin wasn't the only reason you were in the safe house in Kensington, was it. How pregnant were you?'

To Bobbie's surprise, Caroline grinned.

'I knew you were going to be good at this job, Roberta, but I have to say you have surpassed my expectations with this.'

There was a pause while she held up her hand, and as the machine ticked and beeped again, she got her breathing under control.

'I told you I was only in the safe house for a few weeks, but actually it was almost three months, until the baby was born ...'

'And does Colonel Duncan-Browne know about his daughter?'

'I suppose you read his letters as well, did you?'

'No, even I have some scruples. But I did see that you were invited to a ball by a Captain C. Duncan-Browne, and the dates did seem to match up.'

'I'd forgotten that he was only a Captain then, and you would never believe how handsome and charming he was in those days. Sit down again Bobbie, and I'll tell you.'

'I'm sorry Auntie, I should never have …'

'Well maybe not, but you would have wondered about it when you found this,' Caroline clutched the little teddybear to her heart, 'and my other little keepsakes when I'm gone, so it is better that you know.'

'If it is too difficult, I could come back …'

'No just have patience with me and let me catch my breath.'

With the little bear propped up against her laptop, Caroline started to tell her story.

'I made that teddy bear out of scraps of cloth, and knitted the little booties you probably found, while I was bored out of my mind but unable to go anywhere, while in that safe house. I was almost six months pregnant when the cinema got blown up and dear old

Gerald, I mean Colonel Gerald 'Stinker' Forbes fixed it for me to use the safe house. Initially I shared with three other journalists who were involved in the incident in one way or another, and who had also had death treats, but eventually it was just me.
Gerald was the head of Cyril Duncan-Browne's unit in Northern Ireland and responsible for keeping all the press and TV people safe, which meant stopping us getting ourselves into trouble.' There was a pause for breath.
'That was a pretty hard job because we were an unruly bunch and tried every trick in the book to give his men the slip and get closer to the action.'

Caroline smiled at the memory.

'Gerald was good at keeping us under control, though, and second guessing what we might be up to, which is why we called him 'Stinker'.
Cyril Duncan-Browne and I had a couple of dates of a sort, before the Ball, but because we were under military stewardship in what amounted to a war zone, surrounded by fanatical terrorists, all that really meant was a drink in the bar in the barracks.'

'Look, I didn't mean to pry ...' said Bobbie, embarrassed.

'No. I haven't ever told anybody this Bobbie, and it is certainly time that I did.' Caroline picked up the little bear again.
'There was a birthday party in the mess and someone had smuggled some champagne in which we sloshed

about like idiots with gallons of Guinness. I have never had such a hangover in my life as I had the next morning, and although I don't remember much, Cyril …'

Again Caroline paused for breath and they heard the unmistakable sound of the food trolley getting nearer with lunches for the patients.

'So, did he know about the baby?'

'No. No, he didn't. I decided not to ruin his life as well as my own, and I can't say I was in love with him because I wasn't, although I was fairly sure he was trying to nerve himself to ask me to marry him. So I told him I didn't want to see him again, and our group got moved to digs on the other side, in Belfast, a couple of days later. I worked there for a few months before coming back at the time of the the bombing at the cinema. And then we got whisked back to England. I never saw him again.'

'Oh …'

'It was a surprise to me that Gerald, Colonel Forbes, I mean, had remained friends with him and even more extraordinary when he popped up as Geoffrey's neighbour. Life is very strange sometimes.' Caroline sighed and whispered, almost to herself, 'Her ashes are buried in Kensington Cemetery …'

Bobbie helped herself to one of the tissues from the bedside table, dried her eyes and blew her nose.

'That's enough now Bobbie. Go, or you will miss your train.'

As the door opened and the nurse pushed the trolley in, Bobbie picked up her bag and bent to kiss her aunt.

'I love you, Auntie Caroline,' she managed in a broken voice.

'I love you too, Roberta. Now go before it gets messy in here!'

-ooOooo-

Chapter 8

'It is half sunk,' said Pauline. 'No wonder the Coastguard took a while to spot it. I'll email the pictures over.'

'Thank you very much Pauline,' said Bobbie. 'I look forward to seeing them, and it was very kind of you to drive over there, especially as I hadn't realised how far it was.'

'No problem, Buster and I enjoyed the trip. You have to drive quite a long way inland until you can cross the estuary and then back the other side to get to Kilbaha, but there is some lovely scenery on the way that I hadn't seen before.'

'What did you think of the condition of the boat?'

'It was a mess. It was obvious that whoever tried to set fire to it had not entirely succeeded. It is a steel boat, not a fibreglass one, you see, so perhaps there wasn't as much to burn. It was obviously enough to partially sink it though. I arrived just in time to see that the big Coastguard boat that was towing it in was pulling it up out of the water a bit as they got nearer. Then you could see that it was called the "Lady Irene". But when they slowed down and got nearer to the harbour wall it sank down again, so nearly all of it except the wheelhouse was under the water.'

'Did Shaun say if there were any survivors?'

'He said he had been told the Coastguard thought the boat had been abandoned and there was nobody on board.' Pauline lowered her voice almost to a whisper. 'Shall I tell you what I think happened ... I think somebody chartered it for a fishing trip and then shot Eoin O'Grady when they were out to sea.'

'So do I Pauline. And I think they had access to another boat to get away after they had dumped the body in the sea and set fire to the Lady Irene. The question now is can we prove that; and how do we find out who he was in contact with. They didn't find a mobile phone on the body, and presumably that is at the bottom of the ocean now, so the police won't be able to see who he was working with.'

'My bet is it is something to do with the IRA. Who do you think did it, Bobbie?'

'Between ourselves, I think you might be right, Pauline. My aunt told me about that gun-running ship he worked on, that the French captured. If O'Grady was the one who tipped off the authorities, then even all these years later, this could be their revenge. But that must remain between us, Pauline. We must not say a word to anyone until we are certain, including any other press people, because whoever did this is a killer and I wouldn't want to put you in any danger'

'I shan't say a word to anyone. But if you want any more observation work done by a little old lady walking a dog, I shall be delighted to help. It was very exciting, and to be honest life in retirement, even with Buster, can be a bit slow!'

'I'll certainly bear that in mind, Pauline,' chuckled Bobbie. 'And once again thank you very much indeed for making that trip.'

-ooO0oo-

The characteristic shower of gravel on the drive outside told Geoff that Bobbie had arrived, and a glance out of the window confirmed that she was climbing out of her little sports car.

'Hello you,' said Geoff, opening the front door. 'Do you mind if we go to Dorking in the Jag? Bit more leg room.'

'I'll drive very carefully,' said Bobbie.

'No you won't,' said Geoff. 'But this way I pay for the petrol and the old Jag gets a bit of a run, which I have been meaning to give it for ages.'

'All right, Uncle Geoff, if you insist. Have you got the postcode?'

'The what?'

'The postcode, for the sat-nav.'

'Erm, sat-nav wasn't such a popular accessory when the Jag was built, you see and, ...'

'It doesn't have sat-nav? Well I never!'

'I've got a map book ...'

'Doesn't matter, we can use my phone, and actually I'm only teasing. My dear little sports car doesn't have sat-nav either.'

'You little minx ...'

'Shall we be going? I've already entered the address of Hackdoone House on the app, so we're all set.'

-ooOOoo-

Chapter 9

Their visit to Hackdoone House had been very enlightening.

They were met, as they parked just inside the remotely operated gates, by John Parish, the trustee mentioned in the document Caroline had sent to them.

If he could stand, John would have been tall and wiry, but confined to his wheelchair, now with a blanket over the space where his legs should have been, he still cut an impressive figure.

He was smiling broadly as the gates slowly closed behind them, and Geoff could not help noticing the deep scar on his cheek and the tell-tale tram lines indicating extensive stitching, long since healed, along the tanned forearm that he raised now in greeting.

'Welcome to Hackdoone House,' he said in a strong Scottish accent. 'Ah hope you found us without any problems.'

'How do you do,' said Geoff, and immediately regretted it. He should have said something about the weather and kept away from the potential for a long diatribe about this poor man's injuries.

'Never better, thank you. You must be Geoffrey, and this, if I'm not mistaken, must be the famous Roberta.'

'Hello,' said Bobbie, suddenly and uncharacteristically shy.

'Famous?' said Geoff, before he could stop himself.

'Certainly. Many journalists spend their whole careers trying to get a by-line on a story in the Metropolitan Journal, but Roberta here has done it first crack out of the box. That's impressive!'

'Well, it was my Aunt who actually ...'

'No, you are just being modest. Caroline told me all about your heroics when you exposed that big wine scam.'

'Heroics?' spluttered Geoff.

'Um ... please call me Bobbie, Mr Parish ...'

'Only if you'll call me John. Now, would you say it was too early for a wee throat moistener? I have some of our home made cider just ready for tasting, and I'd appreciate your opinion. Follow me ...' And so saying he turned his wheelchair round in it's own length and, moving at a remarkably swift pace that they struggled to match, set off for the main entrance to the buildings.

-oo0Ooo-

Pedro knew that Bobbie was going to Dorking with her uncle this evening, and that he was on his own for supper again.

She had said that she would make herself something when she came home, so not to worry about her. But Pedro always worried about his Bobbie, he couldn't help it.

He had stopped at the supermarket once more to make his choices, but nothing took his fancy. He decided, while trying to think of something healthy to eat that, when you came to think about it, Chinese food was basically just stir-fried vegetables, and what could be healthier than that?

He also knew that Bobbie liked Chinese food and would probably be hungry when she got home, so when the doorbell rang and the courier handed over armfuls of packages which amounted to 'B for 2 with extra beansprouts and a double order of prawn balls,' he expected to receive her thanks and gratitude.

There were rather more packages to deal with than he imagined, and as each dish contained enough for two, rather than being in separate wrappers, he had to almost empty the cupboards of plates and bowls to divide it all up. Then he had the task of deciding what to do with Bobbie's share. He imagined that he would warm it up in the microwave for her when she arrived, but all the dishes would have to be warmed up one by one. While he wrestled with that problem he sat down and ate his own share.

Although it cost rather more than he anticipated, it was very tasty, and he envisaged Bobbie enjoying it and being pleased with him.

Once the separate dishes with all the different types of Chinese food were spread out, there was no room left on the kitchen surfaces or the draining board by the sink. To wash up his own share of the plates and bowls, he had to stack them on the kitchen floor. Then, to add to the volumes he was dealing with he had found that he had quickly become very full and could not finish all of his share.

'Ah,' said Bobbie as she closed the door while Pedro flocked round excitedly saying he had a Chinese feast for her, all ready. 'Uncle Geoff and I were invited into the resident's restaurant in Hackdoone House, so I'm afraid I've already eaten.'

-ooOOoo-

On the phone to her aunt, Bobbie explained what they had learned at Hackdoone House.

'Did you like it?' she asked, when her breathing steadied.

'It was lovely. The gardens are amazing and we met some of the residents when they invited us to join them for supper.'

'And do you think Geoffrey is more settled about being a Trustee now?'

'I think so. John Parish spent some time with us going through the management arrangements and what-not, and he started to relax after that.'

'I'm glad,'

'And some of the residents had really interesting tales to tell. Georgina Marsh was involved in uncovering political scandals and told me all about the time ...'

'I know, Bobbie. I've heard all about it.'

'Oh, yes, I suppose you would have done ... But I think I can learn a lot from these people. Steve Merry worked as a freelance investigative journalist just like us before he had his stroke, and Diana Wilmslow, have I got her name right? ... '

'I think you will find it is Dame Diana Wilmslow, actually,' said Caroline, chuckling.

'Really? Gosh! Well she knows all about computers and databases and worked for the British Secret Service ...'

'Hush now, Bobbie. I'm glad you enjoyed your visit, and I think if you cultivate them, you will find that there is a wealth of knowledge and experience you can draw on at Hackdoone House. So long as John doesn't get you on his cider, of course!'

'How do you know all these people, Auntie Caroline?' Bobbie asked now.

'Well I'm sure they will all be delighted to tell you themselves one day. But did John Parish say anything about that.'

'I was a bit confused about what he said, when I asked him. He said he would have to clear it with you before he told me his story. What did that mean?'

'Dear old John,' laughed Caroline, which bought on a coughing fit.

When her breathing was under control again, she spoke.

'I'm surprised you haven't worked that one out, Roberta, clever girl like you.'

'Pardon?' said Bobbie.

'John worked with me in Ireland. We were both at the abandoned cinema where we were supposed to meet Eoin O'Grady.' As the machines in the background clicked and bleeped, Caroline paused and drew ragged breaths. 'He was very nearly killed in a bomb-blast a couple of months after that. We have been good friends for years.'

'A bomb-blast?'

'Yes. He was lucky to survive. I should have been on the patrol he was on in the Army Land Rover that got blown up. If I had been we would both have been hurt.'

'What stopped you going?'

'Morning sickness,' said Caroline, between deep gasps.

'Oh crikey,' said Bobbie. 'I do know how to put my foot in it, don't I?'

'You certainly have your own way of expressing yourself, Bobbie.' Caroline stopped once more to catch her breath. 'But in a way your direct methods are rather charming, and sometimes the unconventional approach can bring surprising results.'

-ooOOoo-

Chapter 10

'**S**haun is here, Bobbie. Would you like to speak to him?'

'Yes please, Pauline, and thank you.' There was a pause as Pauline handed over her phone.

'Hello? Er, hello, Bobbie. As Pauline said, the autopsy report has come back, and we also got the initial findings from the forensic boys on the boat.' Although Bobbie couldn't see it, of course, Shaun was blushing red and in his embarrassment was unable to keep his feet still so he sat down in a chair in Pauline's sitting room.

'Erm … This is just between us, isn't it Bobbie? The Sergeant doesn't know I'm …'

'Don't worry, Shaun,' purred Bobbie. 'All this is our little secret.'

'Oh, ah. Right,' said Shaun, sinking back into the deep

chair and almost knocking an occasional table flying. 'Good. Yes. Well the autopsy was not much help and didn't say anything we didn't know or couldn't have guessed. O'Grady's face was almost unrecognisable because of the exit wound from the bullet, and they also thought he had taken a considerable beating before he was shot. But the more important stuff came from Forensics looking at the boat.'

'Go on,' said Bobbie, wincing at the thought of a face destroyed by the ballistic effect of an exit wound created by a bullet to the back of the head.

'Well, it seems they pretty much took the boat to pieces and they found several of those floating dry-sacks swimmers use which were tied together in the wheelhouse, and they had traces of drugs inside. If not for finding those they probably wouldn't have stripped it down so much.'

'So this might have been something to do with drugs then?'

'Very probably,' said Shaun, and sounded almost pleased about it.

'I still think it was the IRA,' said Pauline, retrieving her phone from the young policeman.

-oo0Ooo-

Bobbie caught the first train up to Glasgow on Saturday morning and was at the hospital just as the patients were being served a cup of afternoon tea.

'Excuse me,' the nurse at the desk on the entrance to the ward said. 'You are Caroline Bassington's niece, aren't you?'

Bobbie confirmed that she was, and the nurse asked if the Ward Sister could have a word with her before she went in to see her aunt.

Bobbie's unease increased when the Sister, unsmiling and crisp in her dark blue uniform, opened the door to a little side room with armchairs and ushered Bobbie inside.

Although she wanted to speak, Bobbie found her mouth was very dry and she got no reassurance from the nurse's professionally emotionless face as she took the offered seat.

'Roberta, isn't it?' Bobbie nodded in confirmation. 'I shan't keep you a moment but I just wanted to let you know that there has been a bit of a change in your aunt in the last couple of days.'

Bobbie swallowed hard.

'You are aware that she had been becoming increasingly breathless and her speech was becoming more ... more difficult. I'm sorry to tell you that overnight she had a choking incident and we had to sedate her.'

'Oh,'

'She is coming round now and you will find a nurse

is with her to monitor her progress, but we think she may have had a mild stroke, and she has not managed any coherent speech yet.'

'Oh no,' said Bobbie. 'Is she … is she …'

'May I speak plainly, Roberta? Your aunt is quite a remarkably strong lady and has confounded the doctors more than once with her ability to fight back. But you know the prognosis, of course, and this latest incident is, I'm afraid, something of a set back. It is too early to tell if she has definitely had a stroke and how it may have affected her, but she has surprised us with her resilience before.'

Bobbie managed a nod, but found nothing to say.

'So, if you don't mind, please try not to tire her too much today and perhaps keep your visit brief. She is likely to find the difficulty she is having speaking very frustrating and become agitated, and obviously we want to avoid that …'

'Do you think she can still write or type?' Bobbie asked, finding her voice at last.

'I have no idea,' said the nurse, looking alarmed. 'Why? What have you in mind?'

'My aunt,' she said, 'is a skilled communicator. If we can offer her a way to express herself, she may get over this faster.'

'Ah,' said the Sister. 'The notepad, the two mobile

phones and the laptop ... she was a journalist, wasn't she?'

'She _is_ a journalist,' said Bobbie forcefully. 'And if she cannot continue to ... to communicate, I'm sure she will decline rapidly. Can I go and see her now, please. We will see what we can do to help her.'

'Yes, of course. But, I'm sorry Roberta, you do have to face the possibility that this is the beginning of ...'

'Yes, yes. I know. She is in your capable hands, and I'm very grateful of course. But I'm sure she is not giving up yet, so neither am I.'

-oo0Ooo-

'Quite honestly I was really impressed, Janet,' said Geoff. 'Every other nursing home type place I've ever been in was depressing and stank of wee, but this was more like a luxury hotel. There was even a bar in the resident's lounge, and a swimming pool too.'

'A swimming pool in the resident's lounge?' teased Janet.

'No. You know what I mean. And that bloke John Parish is amazing. Quite apart from brewing two different types of very palatable cider, made from the apples in the quite extensive orchard, he also grows vegetables and fruit that he sells to local restaurants.'

'Didn't the thing Caroline sent you say it was a market garden or something before she bought it?'

'Yes, but this John Parish hasn't got any legs and has all sorts of other injuries, but he just won't compromise. He has made all kinds of special tools and hoists and things in a little workshop, so he and other people in wheelchairs can work on the land. He has even adapted a little old tractor they use so that he could drive it and climb up onto it.'

'He sounds pretty amazing.'

'He is, and so are several of the other people we met there. They are not all brain dead zombies sitting about waiting to die. Some of them were younger than me.'

'So do you feel happier about this Trustee thing, now that you have seen it, Geoff?'

'Well, I still want to talk to the lawyer chappy about the legal side of it, but from what I've seen so far, I think it is a magnificent place. I have to admit that Caroline has gone up in my estimation considerably, and to think she set all that up initially with her own money ...'

'Are the buildings modern?'

'Yes, mostly. One bit is only about ten years old, and it all has a really nice atmosphere.'

'No smells, you mean?'

'I mean it is like a cross between someone's rather nice bungalow and a good quality hotel. I wouldn't mind ending my days there one bit.'

'Will you take me with you next time you go, Geoff. I'd like to find out how they deal with some of the health care things, and what they do about going to the dentist.'

'Professional interest aroused, then?'

'I suppose so, yes. I've often wondered what happens about dentistry in that sort of place when the residents can't go out.'

'Surely you know about pulling a tooth by tying a piece of string round it with the other end round the door handle and slamming the door, Janet?'

'Don't be ridiculous, Geoff. What was the food like?'

'Pretty good actually. If you come with me next week when we have arranged to go and meet the manager and some of the staff, they might invite us to lunch perhaps, and you can see for yourself.'

-ooOOoo-

'Hello, my Bobbie,' said Pedro as she answered his call. 'You back the cottage now? Been see the Auntie?'

'Yes. Hello sweetie ... Oh Pedro, she is much worse. They think she has had some sort of a stroke or something. She can't talk, although she keeps trying.'

'Oh. I a sorry hear this.'

'I was with her until supper time, but she can't eat anything in the normal way now, and they have put tubes in to feed her.'

'She no get enjoy the food that way. Is very pity.'

'Yes, but believe it or not, when I realised what she was trying to get me to do, and put one of her mobile phones in her hand ... the hand that she still seems able to use, I mean, she typed on the screen using just her thumb for me to see.'

'What she put?'

'Well several things over a period of time, but the first thing she wrote was "what a lot of fuss!" and that is so typical of her it made me laugh.'

'Still she likes the make laughing then.'

'Yes, and then she asked me to tell her more about the case we are working on and if we met the Manager at Hackdoone House and so on.'

'So is least not too bad, if not all the good then, Bobbie?'

'Well it could be better, of course, but I suppose we have to expect set-backs like this.'

'She ask about the ... the place, you a say? Is this nurse place she build a nice?'

'Hackdoone House? It was brilliant. I was able to tell her that it was not at all what I expected, which I think cheered her up, to be honest. We went on a visit to a nursing home once at Christmas time when I was at school, to sing Carols to the inmates. That was a horrid soulless place and creeped me out, but Hackdoone House was lovely. If you ask me, it is a pity Auntie Caroline is not in there herself.'

'Sing carol's what?'

'Christmas Carols. You know, songs ... "Hark the herald angels sing" ...' chanted Bobbie.

'Oh yays. I get now.'

'Oh Pedro, I hope the herald angels don't come too soon for Auntie Caroline ... I'm going to miss her so very much ...'

-oo0Ooo-

Chapter 11

'So Eoin O'Grady didn't own the boat then, Shaun?'

'No, Pauline. They found out he just rented it occasionally to do his deep sea fishing trips when he found customers. The owner used to do them himself, but he recently got married and moved to Liverpool.'

'So they have tracked him down then?'

'Yes. I saw the email the Liverpool police sent the Sergeant. He lives in a big house outside the town and is something to do with container shipping now, it said. All quite respectable. He is a Parish Councillor and his wife works part-time on a voluntary basis in a charity shop.'

'I see,' said Pauline. 'I wonder where he got the money to buy a big house? There can't have been much of a living in running deep sea fishing trips for tourists in

Kilbaha.'

'Well I don't know the answer to that. But there has also been another report from the forensic people stripping the boat down. They were hoping to find a ship's log or something which would have told them who hired the boat.'

'That would have helped ...'

'But they didn't, although they did find a little clipboard with a slip of paper on it. It wasn't much, I don't think. All it said was "Stevens (3) Girl Sue". No idea what all that meant.'

'Would you like another chocolate digestive, Shaun,' said Pauline. Something about that note had rung a tiny bell, but she could not think what it was.

-ooOOoo-

With Bobbie away in Scotland, Geoff would have been on his own for his next visit to Hackdoone House had Janet not taken the day off work.

'I suppose it will be all right, Geoff. I haven't taken a day off for months and I'm certainly owed some holiday, but I can never help feeling guilty when I'm away from the practice.'

'I'm glad you are coming Janet, apart from the fact that you can look at the map if I take a wrong turn, I think you will really find this interesting.'

'So we are meeting the Manager. What was her name

again?'

'Elizabeth Summers, and we will also meet Gurpreet Gupta, who is the Assistant Manager, I'm told. I've already met the cook, although I can't actually remember her name, and couple of the nurses.'

'Well, shall we hit the road then? Maybe we can find somewhere nice near there for lunch afterwards, if we are not invited into the dining room.'

'I suspect we will be offered lunch, but we will have to see. If not there are plenty of pretty country pubs round there, I think.'

-ooo0oo-

As the visitors were allowed into the wards, Bobbie was in the little florists shop on the ground floor of the hospital waiting while the assistant took what seemed like an inordinate amount of time wrapping the little posy of flowers she had bought.

As Bobbie watched the operation and answered questions about whether she needed a card to go with the somewhat underwhelming floral tribute, she was increasingly disappointed with her purchase.

For the price, in florists away from the hospital, Bobbie could have purchased a very much more substantial, and looking at it now, rather better presented bouquet, but it was too late now.

When it was finally done, and the florist

ceremoniously presented it, as if it was some great work of art, Bobbie snatched it and ran to the lifts.

She may have only lost ten minutes of visiting time, but for Auntie Caroline each minute was precious and Bobbie didn't want to waste even one of them.

-ooOOoo-

'Been thinking,' typed Caroline into her mobile phone screen, as Bobbie watched.

'Reporter golf hotel. Who he.'

After a moment's thought Bobbie got it.

'Do you mean who was the reporter who came to the beach when Pauline Patrick found the body?' She asked.

Caroline raised the busy thumb she had been using to type, then delete, texts for Bobbie to read.

'Pauline gave me his card. I didn't take much notice of it, to be honest. I think he worked for the Irish Times.'

'?offer collaborate?' typed Caroline.

'What, you mean share the story? Why would we do that, we nearly have the whole thing …'

Caroline was typing again.

'Drugs angle. Smuggling locally?'

'Oh, I see,' said Bobbie, 'You think he might know if there is a history of drug smuggling round there. I see.

Other than having found out that there were traces of drugs in bags found on O'Grady's boat, we haven't explored that angle, have we.'

'Boat owner money? Drugs? How pay 4 big house?'

'Yes, Pauline didn't think running a fishing charter would have contributed much to that. I wondered if perhaps he had married a woman with money.'

'Research it!' typed Caroline.

'Yes, auntie,' said Bobbie, aware that she should have thought of that herself.

-ooOOoo-

Chapter 12

Caroline's cottage in Scotland was very old, but had been sympathetically modernised over the years without losing it's charm. The stone walls externally were painted white in contrast to the blue shutters and window frames, and it was set in a small, but secluded garden.

It had two cosy rooms on the ground floor, one of which was presumably originally a dining room but now served as an office, and a long thin country kitchen dominated by an ancient and solid looking breakfast table surrounded by eight wooden 'wheel back' chairs.

There was a modern electric cooker and also a large yellow and black AGA which Bobbie viewed with suspicion and left well alone.

Upstairs there were four smallish bedrooms all of which were partly set into the roof, each with dormer windows. The bedroom Bobbie used was very pretty, in an old fashioned way, and decorated with tiny flowers on the wallpaper which matched the continental quilt cover on the double bed.

The room which Caroline used to store all her papers and which contained the wall of metal banker's boxes, was more stark, with plain painted-over wallpaper and burgundy 'blackout curtains' at the window, and Bobbie was surprised to see that the door had a key operated Yale lock added.

There was only one bathroom, but it did have an efficient electric 'power shower' over the bath and had recently been fitted with modern white sanitary ware.

As Bobbie emerged from the shower this morning, she heard her mobile phone, on charge in her bedroom, ping to register the arrival of a text message, and swathed in towels, she hurried to see what had arrived.

As she grabbed the phone, she saw that the message was to tell her she had missed a call and there was a message on her answer phone.
She keyed in the number to listen to the message and was surprised to hear the voice of her old friend.

'What-ho Bassington, you little beast! Tonya here. Can you give me a call please. Hope you got the invite to the jolly old beano at Belcher Court and can come. The reason I would like to have speech with you is nothing to do with that … more a bit of a wheeze that might interest you and give you and Pedro a bit of a leg up accommodation wise. Hope to hear from you soon. Toodle-oo.'

Bobbie smiled at Tonya's mode of speech, it took her straight back to her school days when all the girls talked like that.

It took her no time to dress and she dialled Tonya's number as soon as she could.

'Toenail?' she said as the call connected.

'Bassington! That was quick. Thanks for calling back.'

'Always a delight to speak to you, Toenail. How can I help?'

'Well, if you are interested, it is more a case of how Giles and I might be able to help you.'

'Go on.'

'Where to begin … You recall of course coming to the office in the London Docklands, where I was all too temporarily employed as a receptionist? But do you remember that I told you the apartment above was the London address of the former Earl of Wymondham, Giles late father?'

'Yes, I remember,' said Bobbie, intrigued.

'Well it emerges that the old buffer also owned a rather splendid town house in St. John's Wood, just round the corner from Lord's Cricket Ground, which until last month was rented out to some distant relative who has been whisked away to live out their days with family. It is rather a grand old place, and Giles and I have decided to tart it up and use it as our London base, rather than the flat over the offices.'

'Very nice,' said Bobbie, wondering what was coming next.

'So, that means that the apartment and for that matter the office on the ground floor is, you might say, surplus to requirements, or, if you prefer, going begging.'

'I see,' said Bobbie, who didn't.

'Well look, the thing is, Giles and I know how much accommodation costs in London, so you could argue that the thing is a bit of a potential money maker, but there is a problem. You see when it was built there was some sort of mis-guided, left wing, job creation scheme in place in that part of the London Docklands, and to get the planning permission to convert the old warehouse it forms part of, the developer had to accept a condition on it to the effect that anyone who occupied it had to be running or working in a local business in the bit downstairs. You will recall the frightful Roland, who ran the office accommodation agency there, that I worked for? That is how we got round the restriction to occupy the flat above.'

'That's rather complicated, I'm not sure I completely understood it. Can you run that by me again?'

'Tut! You were just like this at school, Bassington. Unable to recognise when you were being offered the wheeze of a lifetime, and asking questions while the goose strained to lay the golden eggs. It is quite simple, Giles and I would like to offer you and Pedro the chance to live in the flat in return for creating the impression that the ground floor offices were the hub of your investigative journalism empire. You have to access the flat though the office, which is why it is difficult to separate the two, you see. To deal with the fiscal unpleasantness of this arrangement, if you were prepared to pay us, say, the equivalent of the rent you pay for your little place in Kingston, you could move in as soon as you like.'

'Move in? Pedro and I?'

'Yes, and perhaps I should have explained that the apartment has four bedrooms, or three if use use one as a dining room, two en-suite bathrooms and a cloakroom, and an open plan lounge and kitchen on the top floor with views above the rooftops opposite over the River Thames. Interestingly, if you stand on a chair you can see Tower Bridge from the kitchen and there is quite a big balcony you can sit out on looking out over the river.'

'Blimey!' said Bobbie. 'Are you serious?'

'Never more so, Roberta. There is no point leaving the place empty and Giles would rather see it put to use. Oh, and I should have said ... the apartment and the office are not all there is to the warehouse. The rest of it is a garaging area for two or perhaps three cars and a workshop. There, the original occupant used to create leather belts and things, as far as I can establish. The car parking is obviously useful, but we have never touched the other bit. All that is behind a roller-door arrangement round the other side from the office entrance.'

'That sounds amazing, Toenail. Are you sure about this?'

'Absolutely. You see, if we tried to rent this out as what is known as a "live/work" unit we should have to deal with all sorts of unsavoury types, like the previous Roland, to satisfy the conditions, and we would much rather someone we know was using it. It occurred to me that you, with your little business, fitted the brief like the paper on the wall, and in return for an attractive reduction in rent, you might find a central address handy.'

'Gosh,' said Bobbie, 'this is extremely generous of you, Tonya. But we don't pay anything like the rent a place like that could command, and although we can just about afford the rent in Kingston, there is no way ...'

'Are you not listening, Bassington,' sighed Lady Wymondham AKA Toenail. 'Have I not explained, in terms clear even to your mean intelligence, that the rent you currently pay in Kingston will be more than satisfactory to us as recompense for our warehouse. As an old school friend, I thought you would find the opportunity to your advantage.'

'Oh, I would! Thank you. Thank you very much! I shall have to tell Pedro, of course, but I should think he will be delighted. It is only a short tube ride from there to the bank where he works; and he has finished his college course now so he doesn't need to live in Kingston any more ...' Bobbie was aware that she was gabbling and paused to draw breath. 'Gosh, this is so exciting! Thank you. Thank you very much!'

'Yes, you have said that already, Bobbie. Now, when can I meet you there with the keys to show you round?'

-ooOOoo-

'I hadn't thought of it before we went round to Kilbaha that time,' said Pauline. 'But it was so pleasant for Buster and I to drive out a bit and explore some of the surrounding area that we have decided to do it again on a regular basis.'

'So that is how you ended up in, where was it again? Fenit Marina, down the coast?' said Bobbie.

'Well it is called a marina, but it opens straight out the sea and its more of a little fishing port really.'

'I see.'

'Well anyway, that is where we went, and where we saw this big luxurious cabin cruiser called the 'Girl Sue' coming in and preparing to moor up. I wouldn't have given the ostentatious thing a second glance, had it not been that Constable Shaun said that 'Girl Sue' was the name written on the little clipboard found on the O'Grady boat. Bit too much of a co-incidence, I thought.'

'What did it say on the clipboard again, Pauline?'

'Stevens (3) Girl Sue,' Pauline quoted. 'The funny thing about this is that, I really can't think why, but the name Stevens rang a tiny bell with me as well.'

'I think I might know the answer to that, Pauline. I found the business card of the reporter from the Irish Times you gave me in the bottom of my handbag yesterday.'

'The chap who turned up when I found the body?'

'Yes, that's him. The name on the card was Paul Stevens.'

'Well I never! Yes, now you say that, I remember that was it! You have no idea how much it was niggling at me as to why that name rang a bell. But what does it mean, do you think?'

'Well this is pure conjecture, of course, but it could be that the Girl Sue was the boat O'Grady was expecting to meet him out at sea, perhaps to transfer the drugs he was carrying in those dry-sack things. If so we have one bit of the puzzle.'

'Yes! Of course. So Eoin O'Grady was murdered for

something to do with drugs, then. But why was that reporter involved? How does he fit in?'

'That might have been a co-incidence, perhaps. But if "Stevens" refers to the person who chartered O'Grady's fishing boat maybe he was involved in some way.'

'This Stevens chap was staying in my hotel … I shouldn't keep calling it "my hotel", I only own the buildings, not the business, and I had no idea I owned that until it all came out after Barry, my husband's, death. I'm sorry, what was I saying … oh yes. This Stevens fellow said he was there to play golf when he came down to the beach with the ambulance people, but being a reporter he was naturally interested.'

'You will have to tell me all about your husband and how he came to own that hotel without your knowledge at some point …'

'It sounds awful, but I'm afraid he was living something of a double life and using his insurance commissions to pay for it. I'll tell you about it one day, if you like. It will be nice to be able to talk to someone about it.'

'I'll be happy and interested to hear about that, Pauline,' said Bobbie. 'But first I'd like your views on how Paul Stevens knew the body was on the beach.'

'Probably saw all the Coastguard vehicles and the police car, and of course the ambulance.'

'You said, if I remember correctly, that he seemed to take charge of organising things on the beach, almost as if he knew what he was doing and what to expect.'

'Well, he did seem to be organising people, but some people are just natural managers like that ... the senior partner at the solicitors where I worked did that. He could dominate any meeting and seemed to command respect somehow. Maybe this Stevens was the same.'

'Pauline, can you find out when Paul Stevens booked into your hotel and if he was playing in a golf tournament or meeting people there?'

'Yes. Yes, I suppose I could do that. There is a ledger where they record all the check-ins with times and dates, of course. I wouldn't normally do such a thing but then, come to think about it, the staff do know I own the place, so I could legitimately ask to have a look at that, I suppose.'

'Great,' said Bobbie glancing at her wristwatch. 'Look I've got to go, Pauline, I must not be late for visiting time at the hospital.'

-ooO0oo-

Chapter 13

Caroline was interested to hear all the new details about the case Bobbie had picked up from Pauline Patrick.

'Need buy that dog bone.' she typed into her phone for Bobbie to see.

'Ha! You are right, Auntie. If not for Buster we wouldn't have got this story!'

Bobbie explained that she had not got any further as yet with researching the background of the owner of the Lady Irene or his family. She had asked Pauline to get his name from Policeman Shaun if she could, but until that was to hand, there was not much more that could be done about it.

'OK,' typed Caroline. 'Keep at it.'

'I will, Auntie. I'm afraid I have to go back down to London tomorrow morning, but something else exciting has happened,' and she proceeded to tell her aunt all about her call from Tonya and the apartment in the London Docklands.

'What P think that?' typed Caroline.

'I haven't had time to tell Pedro about it yet, but considering how much easier it will make his journey to work, I should imagine he will be as excited as I am. The only thing that worries me about it is that, from what Toenail says, it is pretty big. Four bedrooms, I think she said. So it might be quite costly to heat and what-not ...'

'Don't look gift horse in mouth,' typed Caroline.

-ooOOoo-

'I told you you would be impressed,' said Geoff as he held open the door of his old Jaguar for Janet. 'My lasagne was delicious. How was your beef stroganoff ?'

'Very tasty indeed,' said Janet. 'I'm glad they invited us to stay for lunch. No wonder the residents of Hackdoone House all look so happy. With catering like that on tap they are having the time of their lives!'

'And talking about "on tap" when I was chatting to John at the bar, he said they were looking into being able to put their sparkling cider into barrels with a tap on the bar for residents.'

'I notice he gave you some bottles to take away ...'

'Yes, very generous of him. I've already put them in the boot.'

'Along with a jar of raspberry jam, a bag of new potatoes, a punnet of strawberries and some carrots, I notice.'

'Yes, well. I thought we ought to buy some of the produce they are selling, just to make something of a contribution ...'

'Thank goodness they don't make their own doughnuts, or I would never have got you away from the place!'

-oo0Ooo-

Bobbie had not liked having to leave her aunt at the hospital, but after a somewhat restless night, she now found herself at the railway station as the express train to London drew in.

As she waited for the train to stop and release the doors, her phone vibrated in her pocket. Fishing it out she saw an email had arrived from Rosy and she decided to wait until she had found her seat to read it.

As she settled, she took the phone out and began to read.

"Isn't it always the way that just when you think things are settling down and everything is going well, the fates conspire to issue the sleeve across the windpipe and dash all one's carefully crafted and meticulously made plans."

Bobbie groaned inwardly and read on.

"Mr Rachman, our landlord, came round to inspect the area in the hall that needed the teeniest bit of re-plastering, after David stripped off the wallpaper. We had already agreed to pay for it and use his preferred plasterer to do the job, so as far as we were concerned the matter was closed and we were just waiting for the plasterer to arrive.

We had not expected Mr Rachman himself to turn up, but lo, when he decided to do so, David had just finished stripping off the ghastly blue and red giant rose wallpaper in the lounge and, unfortunately quite a bit of plaster had come off with that too.

We made it clear we would add this work to that which the plasterer had already been instructed to undertake, and absolutely at our own expense, but Mr Rachman was in no mood to listen to reason and quickly became incandescent.

The upshot is he has told us that we have to stop work immediately and is going to cancel our tenancy. He left saying he was going straight back to his office to issue a 'Notice to Quit' and added that our deposit would be used to pay for the damage.

So, although the lady from Citizen's Advice said we could dispute the notice, she also said that he could nevertheless evict us without much difficulty because we are still in a 'trial period' having only recently taken on the tenancy, so it might not be worth fighting.

So we are more than likely to be homeless very shortly, and with no deposit to use to secure anywhere else!

As you can imagine, David and I are pretty upset about this and not sure where to turn or what to do for the best.

I'm sorry to burden you with my problems, dear old friend of my youth, but if you happen to have any brainwaves do please let us know.

You might have to write to us care of the spot under the canal bridge, but I'm sure your email will find us. Hope things are going better for you.

Rosy."

-oo0Ooo-

As the train slowed at the beginning of it's approach to London Euston station, Bobbie's phone rang and the screen showed that Pauline Patrick was calling.

'Hi Bobbie,' she said. 'I've just got back from the hotel, and I saw Policeman Shaun earlier so I've got some information for you.'

'Brilliant. Thanks Pauline. What have you got?'

'Firstly, Shaun couldn't remember the name of the owner of the Lady Irene, but he just phoned me from the police station where he had looked it up. The chap's name is Conor Doherty and he has also given me his address in Woolton near Liverpool. But the information I got from the hotel is much more interesting ...'

'Go on,' said Bobbie, collecting up her possessions in

readiness to leave the train.

'Right. Paul Stevens booked into the hotel for the four nights before I found the body. He had his supper in the hotel on the first night. He played golf early in the morning of his first full day there with an older man who arrived by car. They only noticed that bit because his guest parked in the Professional's space and he gets touchy about that sort of thing and complained to Mary, the receptionist.'

'OK,' said Bobbie.

'After lunch he played golf again with a young man who also arrived by car. But then it gets really interesting. That night he went out at about half past ten, and when the housekeeper went round early in the morning, his bed had not been slept in. Mary says she thinks she saw him coming in at about half past nine the next morning as she was getting some coffee, and then he seems to have stayed in his room all day.'

'Interesting,' said Bobbie.

'Yes, but that is not all. He was booked in for four nights with the last night being the one after I found the body, but he checked out early so he left soon after the body was found. That is a bit odd because he had another round of golf booked and paid for, for four people, according to the Professional, but none of them turned up to play.'

'Well, that has definitely given me something to think about, Pauline. Once again I must thank you very much for doing all this.'

'Not at all, Bobbie. I am rather enjoying all this. Please don't hesitate to ask me to do anything else you need, and do keep me up to speed with what is happening!'

-oo0Ooo-

Chapter 14

'**I** sorry Bobbie, no had time make the supper.'

'No problem, sweetie. We could go to the pub, if you like. Or get fish and chips. But first there is something I need to talk to you about.'

Bobbie explained all about her telephone conversation with Tonya and the apartment in the London Docklands, and watched as his excitement grew.

'So Tonya is going to be in London tomorrow evening. Is there any chance that you could get over there, straight from work, to meet us at about six o'clock?'

'Yays! Is easy peasy, the get there from the bank. Just the small few stops on the a Tube, and easy walk then. You showing me the map 'sactly where it is. I be there. Hot dog! Is furry citing!'

'I think so too, sweetie, but I must also tell you the news I got from Rosy. That is not good at all.'

Bobbie read Pedro Rosy's email, but was surprised when he interrupted her before she finished.

'Is no problem solve!' he cried. 'Easy peasy. No the problem! You no see the equal, I a mean soldier … er, solution?'

'I don't understand, Pedro. What are you talking about?'

'Is a dead simple, my Bobbie! The Rosy and the David they just got to move in this flat here, when a we move the flash pad in the Dicklands!'

'Docklands,' corrected Bobbie automatically.

'What easier than that? Got the two, three months left on the lease here, and the Rosy she the tenant before with you, so no problema!'

'Good Heavens, Pedro! You are quite right! I've been so wrapped up in work and worrying about Auntie Caroline that I haven't been thinking clearly. Pedro, you are a genius!'

And with that she kissed him smartly on the cheek, reached for her phone and dialled Rosy's number.

-ooo0ooo-

First thing in the morning, after calling the hospital and establishing that there was no change in her aunt's condition overnight, Bobbie was making phone calls.

'Can I speak to Paul Stevens, please,' said Bobbie.

There was a pause.

'Paul Stevens? The reporter?'

'Yes please.'

There was another pause.

'Who did you say was calling again? I need to put you through to the manager.'

There was a third, and somewhat longer pause.

'Hello? Mrs Basinger? My name is Ronan Kelly, I believe you were trying to contact Paul Stevens?'

'Bassington, Miss, actually, and yes please.'

'I'm the department manager. Could you tell me what it is about, please.'

Bobbie thought for a moment and decided to tell a little white lie.

'It is about a story we have been working on together. I have some new information for him.'

'I see. Can you tell me what story?'

'Well, I think I would rather speak to Mr Stevens about it, if you don't mind. We have been working on the story for some time.'

'Oh. Well … erm … the thing is, Paul Stevens is no longer with the Irish Times so …'

'I see. Has he gone to another newspaper?'

'Er, no. He … he is no longer employed here.'

'Ah. Well, to tell you the truth I am not really phoning about a story,' said Bobbie, thinking on her toes and preparing another little white lie. 'I actually work for a recruitment agency and we wanted to offer him a job. From the tone of what you say, can I assume that he will not be getting a reference from your company?'

'Erm …'

There was yet another pause.

'You are probably correct. Perhaps you had better talk to our H.R. Department. This is not really my area.'

'Yes, when exactly was he sacked?'

'On Wednesday … oh dear, I probably shouldn't have said that.'

And with that she put the phone down.

-ooOooo-

More phone calls followed.

'Hi Pauline. Sorry to trouble you again. In the register you were mentioning that they keep on the reception desk at your hotel, do they record the home address and telephone numbers of the guests by any chance?'

'Certainly they do, Bobbie,' Pauline sat up straight in her armchair, which upset Buster who was just getting comfortable on her lap. 'Presumably you are after this Paul Stevens address and what-not.'

'Precisely, Pauline,' said Bobbie, and went on to describe her conversation with the reporter's former employers.

'I wonder if he got the push before or after he came to stay in Ballybunion?'

'Afterwards, I should think, or what would be the point of handing you his business card?'

'Might be a diversion tactic,' said Pauline. 'No, that's nonsense. I've been reading too many spy novels!'

'Perhaps,' said Bobbie kindly. 'But if I can find a way to get him to talk to me ... That is more difficult now, of course. Whilst the original idea of collaborating on the story to share information is obviously not on the cards now, I shall have to think of some other reason for wanting to talk to him.'

'What about saying you work for the hotel and had found some clothes he had left behind or something?'

'That's brilliant, Pauline! Well done.'

Bobbie shook her head in dismay. Why, she asked herself, and not for the first time today, had she not thought of that herself.

'The other thing I thought of,' said Pauline now, 'was that you might need to know what he looks like. Would you like me to get hold of the CCTV footage from the reception and the carpark area from when he was there?'

Bobbie had not thought of that, either.

-ooOOoo-

Chapter 15

At ten minutes to six Bobbie was standing outside the former offices of Wider World Wines which she had first visited with her aunt, when they were investigating a big international wine scam.

She was excited and kept looking around her to see if Pedro was coming along the road.

In front of her was the rather ordinary entrance to an office which stood in stark contrast to the style of the rest of the building it occupied.

Built for purely industrial purposes in Victorian times, the square red brick building was originally plain and purposeful, and might even be described as austere. Now however it was somewhat uncomfortably hung about with what, in the 1980's seemed to the developer who bought it, to be age appropriate embellishments. This ornamentation was designed, no doubt, to make it look more like the trendy warehouse conversions further along the road, where apartments sold for astronomical prices.

High up, above a plain arched window, an imitation 'lifting wheel', probably made of fibreglass, had been added. Lower down artificial lead 'fire insurance plates' had been added to tell long since defunct Victorian private fire services that the building could be extinguished, with all bills paid, should it catch light. On one corner a dull red painted angled bracket with a black chain thrust out purposefully over the street. In the eye of the beholder, it hinted at some task it may once have been put to, but certainly not since the architectural salvage yard it was no doubt acquired from had sold it.

Now, as she watched, a florescent tube light was flickering into life behind the glass office door and her friend Tonya appeared, framed in the doorway and beckoned her in.

'Bassington, you found us! Why are you loitering there? Not waiting for Pedro, I hope. He has been here for the last twenty minutes!'

-oo0Ooo-

'Yays, is furry luxury, David,' agreed Pedro as they settled at the table in the pub. 'Got the big a balcony see the river, and even the little small lift go down the basement carpark!'

'Convenient for work too,' said David, taking another

deep draught of his pint.

'Sure thing, you betcha. Is just the steps from a the tube station, don't even have to change. Easy peasy. Bobbie, she likes the furnace … ah no, mean furniture, too, so is no need spend the big money. Only we taking the bed we got. I sorry, but is new and not leaving behind.'

'No problem,' laughed David. 'As it happens we bought a new bed when we moved into Putney, so that works well.'

'How we move them?'

'I think we should hire a van and use it to move our stuff from Putney to your flat in Kingston, and then your stuff from Kingston to the Docklands place.'

'Is need be the big one … The Bobbie she got many books and a plenty clothes, also the many shoes …'

'That's alright, I can probably get one or two of the lads from my rugby club to help us with the humping …'

'What you need help with the humping?'

'Yes, carrying the heavy stuff.'

'Oh sorry, for moment I think you meaning …'

'Hello playmates,' bellowed Rosy, returning to their table. 'Empty glasses, I see. I'm sure Bobbie and I can soon attend to that!'

-ooo0ooo-

'This raspberry jam is delicious,' said Geoff, spreading a little more on his scone. 'I'm going to get some more next time we go to Hackdoone House.'

'I haven't tried that yet, leave some for me,' said Janet.

The weather was so delightful that, it being a Saturday, Geoff and Janet had decided to take their afternoon tea outside, and Geoff, having wrestled with a folding table which he erected on the terrace, was contentedly tucking into the scones they had bought from the supermarket earlier in the day.

'Hello?' called a voice. 'Anyone home?'

'Its Duncan-Browne,' hissed Geoff. 'Quick! Hide the scones!'

But he was too late, as around the corner of the garage Retired Colonel Cyril Duncan-Browne appeared.

'I thought I could hear voices. Been ringing the bell but realised you must be in the garden on such a smashing day. How are you both?'

'Very well, thank you Cyril. And you?' said Janet politely.

'Oh, top hole, thank you. Never better … Are those scones you have got there? Raspberry jam?'

'Oh all right,' mumbled Geoff resignedly.

'Yes, would you like one?' said Janet in her brightest voice.

As Cyril settled in the chair Geoff fetched for him and Janet poured him tea, he began to explain the reason for his call.

'So you see, as a result of our arrangements with the fishing club, we have the chance once again to fish some salmon water in Scotland, and if you are interested ...'

'Oh rather!' said Geoff, offering their visitor the spoon and the raspberry jam.

'Whereabouts would this be?' asked Janet. 'I'm wondering if I could come too and do a bit of sight-seeing. I've only been to Scotland a couple of times, and I'd like to see a bit more of it.'

'I'm sure that could be arranged,' said Duncan-Browne. 'I don't know this particular area myself but it is quite near somewhere called the Trossachs Locks, apparently, and Carron Valley Reservoir, which is mostly brownies and rainbows. The best bit, from a fishing point of view is supposed to be by something called the Potts of Gartness on the River Endrick, where there are salmon and trout to be had from July, apparently.'

'We will have to do a Google search of the area,' said Janet. 'But if it is near somewhere interesting, apart from just the fishing, I mean, I would like to come.'

'I don't know about tourist attractions except that, in Killearn, there is a distillery you can visit, but it is all very picturesque from what I'm told. We do have to find our own accommodation this time, Geoff, but if you are interested ...'

Geoff was smiling broadly as he offered Duncan-Browne another scone.

'Yes please!' he said.

-ooO0oo-

Bobbie phoned the hospital for an update and was told there was no change in Caroline's condition.

She asked the nurse to tell Caroline that she would be up to see her on Tuesday and would stay until Friday. Next Saturday, if all went well, they would be moving house, if they could find a suitable van to rent.

There was so much to do before then.

The landlords of their Kingston flat, who lived on the ground floor of the converted house, had to be told that Rosy would be moving in with David, and she and Pedro would be leaving. They were a nice old couple, and so long as their income from the flat was uninterrupted Bobbie was sure they wouldn't mind.

Geoff and Janet had to be told, and change of address emails, cards and notices had to be prepared for friends, relatives and banks and so on.

Bobbie had telephoned her mother who seemed quite pleased and promised to come up and see them once they were settled.

She had also fought her way through the difficult and complicated business of telling the gas and electricity suppliers, the local councils at both ends, and her college, although her work there was pretty much at an end, and she had just submitted her last essays.

Those essays were only slightly late and her tutor had assured her it did not matter. She made sure that they had the new address which hopefully they could use to send her the Certificate and her invitation to the graduation event after the holidays.

With a sigh, she sat back in her chair at the battered kitchen table and then, having decided that she was ready to get back to work, she tried to ring the former reporter, Paul Stevens number. There was no reply.

-oo0Ooo-

Chapter 16

Ploughing through the CCTV files Pauline had sent through was extremely dull. They took ages to download and even longer to watch, even when speeded up to the maximum.

Bobbie found her head nodding and her eyes closing on several occasions and had to jerk herself awake and make yet more coffee at regular intervals. Finally, however, she thought she had found something worth watching.

She slowed the blurry picture until it was running at four times normal speed, and when the recording reached 22:18 on the day before the murder she stopped it. This showed Paul Stevens walking past the reception desk and out onto the carpark with a large backpack in his arms.

Bobbie found the equivalent time on the CCTV download of the car park and watched him coming out of the door and getting into a black car which immediately drove off.

There was no further sign of him until 09:26 the following morning when what looked like the same black car drove up and dropped him off outside the hotel door, this time without his backpack.

The angle of the camera made it impossible to see the number plate of the car except for the tiniest moment, when it turned out of the drive, then perhaps, Bobbie decided, she could make out a 'W' and a '5' or perhaps an 'S', but that was all.

She decided it was time she saved the relevant sections of footage to a file and emailed them back to Pauline, who could send them on to Constable Shaun.

How relevant Paul Stevens was to the investigation she had no idea, but she reasoned, the fact that he checked out early from the hotel and missed his paid for round of golf; and then his nocturnal movements, along with the subsequent loss of his job, certainly did not add up to normal behaviour. Maybe Constable Shaun could shed some light on it.

-ooo0oo-

'You have just missed Shaun,' said Pauline. 'He called round to say that the Coastguard have got hold of some satellite footage which shows the Lady Irene before it caught fire.'

'Really? That's interesting.'

'Yes, Bobbie. And that is not all. Shaun said it shows another bigger boat alongside, which had approached from the south.'

'Another boat?'

'Yes. Shaun says it is this bigger boat and others like it that the Coastguard were actually tracking. The Customs people had taken an interest in it, apparently and thought it might be up to no good.'

'And did this take place late at night?'

'Yes, and that is why it is so relevant. The two boats seemed to be together at about one o'clock in the morning, and then the bigger boat moved away about half an hour later.'

'What did they think they were doing?'

'Well, you have to remember that Shaun is only a very junior local policeman and is not likely to be involved in high level discussions about this, but he did say that he got the impression that this was something to do with drug smuggling.'

'I thought it might be,' said Bobbie.

'Shaun also said that he had been told to go down to Kilbaha with the Sergeant and interview the locals to see if they saw anything.'

'I thought they had been told to do that some time ago.'

'They were, and apparently the Sergeant got a bit of a ticking off for not doing it.'

'Probably a bit late now …'

'Yes, but that reminds me. It is probably nothing at all, but Shaun said the reason they had not been over there before was because there had been a couple of car thefts, including the Mayor's wife's car, which the Sergeant regarded as more important. I'm not actually sure about this, but Buster and I went on a drive over to Lisselton for our walk this morning and when we were walking down past the old industrial estate there on our way back to the car, I think I may have seen the Mayor's wife's car.'

'Really?'

'Well, as I said I can't be sure, but the Mayor's wife's car is a brand-new Mazda in a very distinctive shiny red colour, and I've seen her swanking about in it in the town several times. Anyway, there was quite a strong gusty wind, and as we were walking past on the other side of the road, a man was struggling to close one of the doors on an old car repair place against the wind. As the door blew open I'm pretty sure I caught a glimpse of that car inside.'

'Have you told Shaun?'

'Yes, and he couldn't wait to get back to the station to tell the Sergeant.'

'Let's hope you were right ... that will be a feather in Shaun's cap.'

'Yes, but he might have to explain where he got the information, and that might reveal how much time he spends round here ...'

-ooO0oo-

The area around the Trossachs Locks, the River Eldrick and the little town of Killearn looked very pretty, at least in the internet searches Janet had done with Geoff sitting at her side.

'In terms of accommodation, there are various hotels we could stay in, Geoff, but none of them are cheap and, depending on the actual dates we can go, they look pretty booked up.'

'Yes, Janet, I saw that. When we went to Scotland salmon fishing before, we stayed in a lovely little B&B which was very reasonable and set up for people fishing. Are their none of those available?'

'Yes, there are a couple. I rather like the look of this one in Killearn,' she pointed at the property in question on the screen.

'Very nice. You know I can't think why, but the name Killearn rings a bell with me ... hang on! I've got it! That is where Caroline Bassington lives! I'm sure of it.'

'Really? What a pity she is so unwell, she might have been able to recommend some accommodation around there.'

'Yes. I notice it is near Glengoyne Distillery and they do guided tours. Duncan-Browne will like that.'

'Yes, and not far from Loch Lomond. I should like to visit that,' said Janet.

-ooOOoo-

'That's right a Luton van, he said,' enthused Rosy. 'It is owned by someone my Uncle Peter knows. Something to do with horse racing, I think.'

'I haven't met your Uncle Peter, have I?' asked Bobbie.

'Bless you, no! You would not have been able to forget Uncle Peter, try as you might,' chuckled Rosy. 'He is something of a blot on the family escutcheon, and regarded as rather a pest by the senior members. I adore him, enormous white moustache and all!'

'So what have we got to do again?'

'We have to meet him at Sandown Park Racecourse in Esher early on Saturday morning, and he will introduce us to the chappie who is going to lend us the van. From what Uncle Peter says it is plenty large enough to handle removals and we could possibly do the whole thing in one trip.'

'Well that will be good.'

'Yes and David's rugby club chums will be waiting for us in Putney when we get there to load it all up, so all we have to do is drive the van there.'

'And I meet you at Esher railway station?'

'Correct. Obviously our cars will be in the wrong place if we drive and Sandown Park Racecourse literally adjoins the station. Uncle Peter said he would meet us by the gate to the first car park just along the road.'

'Right.'

'I could have gone on my own, I suppose, but I'd rather not, if you don't mind. I'm not expecting you to contribute to the fifty quid this chappie wants, by the way … it is the least we can do after your kindness in rescuing us from sleeping under the canal bridge.'

'I'm sure it wouldn't have come to that, Rosy. We would have worked something out.'

'Well perhaps, but as it turned out, things really are looking up and couldn't have been better.'

'I'm glad you look at it like that, Rosy.'

'Yes. Now we have a car, getting to work even from the distant rolling suburbs of Kingston-On-Thames is not going to be too bad …'

'I hope your car fits in the space my dear little sports car goes in on the drive. It is very narrow.'

'I'm sure we will manage to elbow our way in, Bobbie. That is the least of our problems.'

'Right. The train station at Esher, then. See you there

on Saturday.'

-ooOOoo-

Chapter 17

Travelling again to Scotland, Bobbie used the time to review where she was with the case.

If Pauline had actually spotted the Mayor's wife's car when walking Buster, and if Shaun got to claim the credit, that was a good thing, and also removed the obstacle to the police taking statements in Kilbaha. She wasn't sure that anything much would come of that, but you never knew.

Very little seemed to be known about Eoin O'Grady's use of the Lady Irene between contracts on container ships. She remembered that they now knew who owned the boat, but they had no information about this Conor Doherty, and it was difficult to establish how it was that he went from charter fishing boat skipper to containership magnate with a big house in a posh suburb of Liverpool. Perhaps he married money.

And what about this satellite image the Coastguard had got of another boat alongside the Lady Irene. Was that the Girl Sue, and if so what were they doing? Was it a drugs pick up, perhaps?

Caroline had stressed that allowing your imagination to run away with you was a great risk for an investigate journalist, and that creating scenarios in your head as to what happened was natural, but best avoided, or at least carefully controlled. The facts had to fit the story, Caroline had counselled. But what facts were there to play with here?
Precious few, sighed Bobbie.

And what of this Paul Stevens? Was his unusual behaviour at the hotel anything relevant? Maybe he went to see a girlfriend. That would account for his absence from the hotel. But then, why had he lost his job, and why didn't he stay to play the round of golf he had paid for before he left Pauline's hotel.

So, going back to the beginning, what do we know about Eoin O'Grady?

Presumably, as he was working on the Eksund, involved in running weapons at least once, he was an IRA sympathiser, although he was very young when he had that job.

What about the IRA angle? Did O'Grady tip the authorities off about what the Eksund was carrying and could this be their revenge, all these years later?

Surely that was quite an interesting story in itself, and yet the Irish Times was the only newspaper to even mention the discovery of the body on Ballybunion beach, and they only gave it one short paragraph hidden away on page three.

Her Aunt Caroline's time in Ireland and the fire-bombing of the old cinema tied the story together and made the historical context interesting, but it didn't explain everything.

Bobbie sighed, and to distract herself, turned to the pages in her notebook where she had made lists of all the things she had to do to prepare for her move to the London Docklands at the end of the week, but the lists danced before her eyes and she could not concentrate.

-ooO0oo-

One of the advantages of today's modern express trains is that they have fairly reliable wi-fi, and searching the internet is possible. Mobile telephones have good signals too, most of the time, so working on a train is actually a reasonably practical proposition.

Bobbie had tried ringing Paul Steven's number three more times so far on this journey. But there was no reply, and no answering machine, so she was not getting anywhere.

For want of something else constructive to do while she took a break, she 'googled' The Girl Sue, the luxury cabin cruiser Pauline had seen coming into the marina in Ireland, and which was named in the note on the little clipboard found on Eoin O'Grady's boat.

There were several boats with similar names on the internet but only one which was recognisably a luxury cabin cruiser and based in southern Ireland. Bobbie saw that 'The Girl Sue' was available to charter with a crew, and had its own website.

On that website, along with the pictures of the admittedly rather lovely boat, draped with suitably stylish men holding glasses of champagne and decorative bikini clad women, presumably taken on trips to the Mediterranean, there were details of how to hire the vessel.

The Girl Sue, she read, was owned by a consortium of businessmen headed by one owner who took responsibility for bookings. Bobbie almost dropped the paper cup of coffee she was holding as she read that bookings could be arranged through a Mr Finn Stevens and listed his contact details.

The postal address was the same as the one Pauline had copied out from the hotel register, although the telephone number listed was a 'land-line' rather than a mobile phone.

Bobbie set her coffee aside and drew out her notebook. She must think carefully how she was going to approach this she thought, and as the train lumbered on, she started to write down ideas.

-ooo0ooo-

Bobbie was dismayed to see that Caroline was linked up to more machines as she entered her room in the hospital. She looked very small as she reclined on the bed, propped into a semi-sitting position, with tubes in her nose under a mask and wires seeming to sprout from under her nightdress at all angles.

Bobbie noticed straight away that she still had one of her mobile phones in her hand and a cable from it led to a charger. Her makeshift desk, with her laptop and notepads had been pushed aside and now sat at an angle beside a new machine with cables and tubes running to the bed.

The television had also been pushed out of the way, and the little device Caroline had connected to it to control it sat on the notepad beside her laptop.

Caroline opened her eyes as Bobbie entered the room and she typed 'Hi' on her mobile phone screen, followed by the word 'update.'

Bobbie asked if she wanted an update on the case, and after a short pause, Caroline raised her thumb.

'Are you in any pain?' Bobbie asked, before they went any further.

'No drugged.' Caroline typed.

'Is there anything you need, auntie?'

'Update,' typed Caroline.

Bobbie smiled as she recognised a fleeting glimpse of the twinkle in her aunts eye which indicated amusement.

'Right,' she said. 'So here is the news …'

-ooOOoo-

Chapter 18

Her time with her aunt on this occasion was somewhat subdued and communication was certainly getting more difficult. Caroline's responses were limited to one or two words of text and sometimes there were long gaps before she pressed any keys on her mobile phone.

The nurse, who popped into the room every twenty minutes or so, continued to express her support for Caroline's continued efforts but at one point, when Bobbie was returning from a call of nature and the nurse caught her in the corridor, she did have something to say.

'I'm sure Caroline wants to continue to do this, but it is obviously tiring her. I think you should let her rest now and perhaps try again tomorrow, if you can still be here. If she gets over stimulated it could trigger another incident.'

Before Bobbie could help herself she had reacted.

'No! You don't understand. In her own way my Auntie Caroline is still working. It is all she lives for. Take that way from her and … and.' And to her dismay and embarrassment Bobbie found that she had collapsed into tears.

The nurse steered Bobbie into the little anti-room with the armchairs, passed her the tissue box from the table, and sat down next to her with a hand on her arm.

'Can I call you Bobbie like Caroline does?' she asked; and wiping her eyes, Bobbie nodded.

'I know this is incredibly hard, Bobbie, and you are being amazing about it, particularly as you live so far away and have to keep travelling back and forth, but I'm afraid it is not going to do any good, you know.' The nurse squeezed her arm. 'My name is Emma by the way and I've worked on this ward for three years now, so I know how this goes.'

Bobbie looked properly at the nurse for the first time, and took in her kind eyes and comfortable features. She noticed a gentle smile and wished that this kindly soul was allowed to give her a cuddle.

'You probably haven't noticed, but I have been timing Caroline's responses and looking at what she writes. Have you noticed that she answers questions, increasingly with a "Y" or an "N", but doesn't ask questions now. It is true that you are getting responses from her, but they are getting less meaningful.'

Bobbie wanted to deny this observation but, now that it had been drawn to he attention, she had to admit that the nurse was right.

'I've never known anyone to use a mobile phone before to make responses like this and it is certainly something that the doctors have been talking about. Maybe other patients will be offered their mobile phones to see if they can use them in the same way in the future, so you aunt has possibly helped other people. But that is not really the point here, Bobbie.'

'What do you mean,' sniffed Bobbie.

'Can I speak plainly?'

'I wish someone would. Tell me the truth, please.'

'All right. The machines are keeping your aunt's body functioning, Bobbie, and her mind is beginning to slow down too. You must see that.'

Bobbie nodded and blew her nose.

'It could be today, or tomorrow or next week when her body stops being able to support her mental functions as well. She is unbelievably tough and quite frankly has astounded the doctors up until now, but inevitably that is starting to change.'

'She said she wasn't in any pain …'

'We have done all we can to make sure of that, but while the medication slows everything down, we can only give palliative care now.'

'I know,' sniffed Bobbie. 'I just don't want ...'

'I know, I know ...' said Emma, and probably breaking all sorts of hospital rules, gathered Bobbie in her arms and held her tight.

-ooO0oo-

Back in Caroline's cottage, Bobbie composed an email to Pauline Patrick.

"Hi Pauline," she wrote. " I'm up in Scotland at the moment, but I've discovered something that I think the police need to know about and I thought you might like to pass it on to Shaun.
I have found out that The Girl Sue, the big luxurious cabin cruiser you saw at Fenit Marina is owned by a consortium of businessmen headed by a Finn Stevens and his address is the same as the one Paul Stevens gave and you got from the hotel register.
I attach a link to the rather flash website which gives details of how to charter the Girl Sue with a crew.
I can't prove this, but I now think that the boat shown on the satellite image the Coastguard got is The Girl Sue which was clearly meeting up with the Lady Irene. I think Paul Stevens and two others (hence the (3) on the clipboard the police found on-board) may have chartered the Lady Irene to take them out to sea, possibly to pick up some drugs dropped there by

another ship. Maybe this happened regularly, maybe not, but either way the collection of those 'dry sack' things tied together with traces of drugs does prove that drugs came into this somehow.

Possibly Paul Stevens plan was to meet the Girl Sue but Eoin O'Grady may not have known that was the idea. Could it be that the crew of the Girl Sue, headed by Finn, who must be some relation of Paul Stevens as they share the same address, boarded the Lady Irene to steal the drugs from the drop and in the process beat up and shot Eoin O'Grady and then tried to sink his boat to hide what they had done?

The flaw in that theory, and it is only a theory at this stage, is that I can't think what they had to gain by killing O'Grady and sinking his boat. If the intention was just to pinch the drugs, they could have done that without committing a murder as well. Also the way O'Grady was tied up does not fit well with that idea. Why bother?

Anyway, the thing for Shaun is the news about the ownership of the Girl Sue, which I suspect he will need to pass on to someone senior up the line. Presumably that would be a detective allocated to the case, but we obviously don't know who that is, unfortunately.

With apologies for the length of this email, please give my best to Shaun.

Regards,

Bobbie"

She sighed as she clicked 'send', maybe she should not have bothered Pauline with her ideas as to what may have happened, but it felt good to have written it all down, and it had helped her to get the sequence sorted out in her own mind.

-ooOOoo-

Bobbie was always rather suspicious of calls which caused the words 'No caller ID' to appear on the screen of her mobile, so she was ready to hang up quickly if it turned out to be just another scam call.

'Hello, is that Bobbie Bassington?' said the caller, and as nobody trying to sell her anything was likely to know her nickname was Bobbie, she answered that it was.
'This is Detective Sergeant Mike Rowbotham from Killarney police in County Kerry, Ireland. Young Shaun at Ballybunion has given me your number.'

'I see,' said Bobbie. 'How do you do?'

'Very well thank you. Now young Shaun has shown me your email and told me about your investigation into the shooting of Eoin O'Grady and I think you might be able to help us out.'

'Well, I'm always happy to help the police, of course,' said Bobbie.

'That's the right spirit. Can I just run through a couple of questions so I know who I'm dealing with, and then perhaps we can get our heads together on this one. Firstly, though, can I ask if you are anything to do with Caroline Bassington the journalist?'

Bobbie explained the connection.

'I met your aunt many years ago and have a huge respect for her work, she is a remarkably resourceful journalist who has helped us in various investigations I was involved in back in the day.'

'Auntie Caroline does seem to have met people everywhere,' said Bobbie. 'It never fails to astonish me how well connected she is.'

'Yes, well. If I could just work through these identity questions, purely routine stuff, but we have to do these things by the book ...'

'Of course,' said Bobbie and answered the string of questions.
'I have one question for you before we get started,' she said. 'Could you tell me how you come to know my aunt?'

'Certainly,' said the policeman. 'I first met Caroline in the late 1980's or early 1990's when she was working for an English newspaper based in Belfast and I was a very junior constable assigned to work with the British Army as a trainee liaison officer. She was in the group of journalists we were assigned to keep out of trouble, alongside some Army officers.'

'I see. So you go back a long way then.'

'Oh yes. That was my first posting, and I'm coming up for retirement now, so it feels like a lifetime ago.

She was always very good to us, but I have to say she was also always giving us the slip and dashing off somewhere after a story or an interview and we spent as much time trying to find her as we did looking after her!'

'That sounds just like my aunt!' chuckled Bobbie.

'Yes, well. Could we perhaps have a few words about Eoin O'Grady now, please.'

What followed was something of a revelation for Bobbie, especially when the policeman said, 'I suppose you knew that the IRA had a contract out on Eoin O'Grady and each of the crew members of the Eksund who are still alive, offering quite serious money to anyone who could locate them? Of course this also proves that the IRA have never identified which of the crew betrayed the Eksund and its cargo of weapons to the French police, so they had to issue a contract on all of them.'

'That's it!' said Bobbie.

'I beg your pardon?' said the policeman.

'I said "that's serious" about the contract, I mean,' said Bobbie.
The fact was she had just realised where Paul Stevens the former Irish Times journalist fitted into the picture. He must have found out who Eoin O'Grady was and discovered his whereabouts.

The slightly sinister thing about this realisation was

that it would appear that Paul Stevens, having found him, had intended to hand O'Grady over to the IRA, and presumably collect a payment for his trouble.

-ooOOoo-

Chapter 19

On Friday afternoon, as she boarded the train back to London, Bobbie noticed that there were more people travelling than she had experienced before. She had to fight her way down the central aisle to get to her seat amongst all the cases and people trying to find space for their possessions.

Within sight of her reserved seat, the train lurched as it left the station, and she almost fell over an inconsiderately placed suitcase. A kindly elderly gentleman caught her arm and prevented an unseemly tumble.

'Ow,' said Bobbie rubbing a barked shin, and to the man, 'Thank you very much.'

'No problem. Are you OK?'

'Yes, thanks to you,' said Bobbie. 'Really crowded today, isn't it.'

'Is that your seat?' said the man, pointing. 'Here let me help you.' and needing no further encouragement he politely asked a enormously fat and sweating woman fighting with a holdall to excuse him and steered Bobbie and her bags towards the table and the spot she had reserved.

'Phew! Thanks,' said Bobbie collapsing into the seat.

'A pleasure. I'm just one row back there if you need any assistance at the other end or as we go along,' he said, and with a wide smile he moved back to his seat.

It is strange how little acts of kindness can affect the human psyche and Bobbie found, to her dismay, that she was finding it hard not to cry.

She had not wanted to leave her aunt's bedside this time and had a great sense of foreboding.

Caroline's text responses had become slower and slower and she seemed to fall asleep every few minutes. When Emma, the nurse, was there when this occurred, she said to just hold her aunt's hand and sit quietly.

When she seemed to be awake, however, Bobbie found herself prattling away about the case and explaining everything that had happened as if nothing had changed.

At one point, when Caroline was awake and seemed to be a little more aware of what was going on, she unexpectedly wrote the word 'Bobbie' on her mobile, but although Bobbie assured her she was there, her aunt added nothing further and fell into another doze.

When Bobbie had to come away and said goodbye, her aunt smiled slightly but added no further words on her screen, and nurse Emma, seeing that, walked out with Bobbie as she made to leave.

'Have we got your mobile number, Bobbie,' she said as they reached the end of the ward.

'Yes. If I can get a flight, I can be here in about three hours,' said Bobbie choking back the tears. 'It's not going to be long now, is it ...'

'I'll stay in touch,' said Emma, squeezing her hand. 'Safe travelling.'

-ooOOoo-

On the train Bobbie took a call from Pauline Patrick.

'Hi Bobbie. I was right about the Mayor's wife's car it seems, and an arrest has been made. Shaun got congratulated for that by his superiors who said it was a good example of community police work!' Pauline chuckled. 'Good bit of dog walking, I'd say! Shaun is here and wants a word ...'

'That's right. Hello Bobbie' said Constable Shaun, 'Colin Patterson Seafreight have at last got back to us with some information. Eoin O'Grady had just finished a four month tour with them.'

'I see,' said Bobbie.

'And the interesting thing was that, on the last voyage, the ship got a visit from the Coastguard. It was about a drug drop that they had a tip off was due to take place out to sea off Ireland. The way that works, apparently is the smuggler on the container ship drops drugs in floating packages at a set location and they are picked up later by a small boat and taken, sometimes to Ireland, but mostly to the mainland along the Liverpool coast.'

'Did they make any arrests?'

'Not this time. Nothing was found, so they wondered if the drop had either already taken place, or they got the wrong ship.'

'Could that have been the packages found on the Lady Irene with traces of drugs?'

'Possibly, but there was no sign of the actual drugs, and the Lady Irene would have been at, or beyond the limits of its capabilities, that far out into the Atlantic. The Coastguard guy that the Sergeant spoke to thought they would need a bigger boat in the seas out there.'

'Shaun, do you think it is possible that the Girl Sue was that bigger boat?'

'I suppose it could have been. It is a lot more

seaworthy and capable than a little inshore fishing boat like the Lady Irene, perhaps.'

'Weren't the Coastguard tracking the Girl Sue when it met up with the Lady Irene?'

'I thought they were watching them and some other similar boats to see if there was any booze or cigarette or maybe people smuggling going on. You get a lot of that off this coast.'

A voice in the background spoke up.

'Did you know that smuggling booze and that sort of thing was a major contributor to how the IRA got their funding.'

'Thanks, Pauline,' said Bobbie.

'Bobbie says "thanks Pauline",' said Shaun.

'I've been reading up about that,' called Pauline, 'I found out that the IRA did not like drug dealing as it upset their Catholic supporters, so generally, at least, that is not how they made their money.'

'I see,' said Bobbie. 'Thanks again.'

-oo0Ooo-

As the train rattled on, Bobbie sat with her notebook open at a new page and started writing.

Girl Sue connected to Paul Stevens who probably told the IRA about finding Eoin O'Grady. His relative Finn is in charge of Girl Sue.

Was Lady Irene picking up from a drugs drop … could it get that far out into the main shipping lanes.

Girl Sue and Lady Irene together … why?

'Hang on!' thought Bobbie. 'Supposing the Girl Sue's passengers were IRA sympathisers and Paul Stevens, having chartered the Lady Irene, was delivering Eoin O'Grady to them to collect his reward. Then supposing the Girl Sue picked up the drug drop, and then went on to meet with the Lady Irene, where they shot O'Grady.'

Bobbie sucked the end of her pen.

'Yes, of course!' she told herself. 'Then the crew of the Girl Sue put the floating drug bags on the Lady Irene to make it look like the Lady Irene had picked up the drugs!'

She wrote in her notebook again.

But the drug bags were empty. Where were the drugs?

Paul Stevens must have escaped on the Girl Sue … must find out what relation Finn Stevens is to him.

Where is Paul Stevens now?

-ooO0oo-

On Saturday morning Bobbie was alighting from another train, but this one was almost empty, and she had Rosy for company.

As they had been told, Sandown Park Racecourse

adjoined the platform at Esher, and on leaving the station it was but a short walk to the first carpark entrance to the racecourse.

There they met a tall, slim, elegantly turned out older man with a luxuriant white moustache. This, Bobbie was told, was Uncle Peter, who Rosy embraced joyfully.

'What a delight to see you after so long, Rosy, my dear. And this, if I am not mistaken, must be the lovely Bobbie, of whom I have heard so much!' And he gently raised Bobbie's hand to his lips, and said, 'Charmed, charmed.'

Trying not to giggle at his olde world manners, Bobbie said 'How do you do?'

'Tip-top, thank you young lady, and all the better for making your acquaintance.'

'Yes, well. I had better warn you, Bobbie, that Uncle Peter here is sometimes as young as he feels, and most of the time that is about twenty-two. Down Uncle, down I say!'

Uncle Peter's twinkling eye caught Bobbie amidships as he chortled loudly.

'Rosy is quite right. I am an incorrigible old blighter and probably should be behind bars. But whilst I am still at liberty to roam free I refuse to be anything but merry and bright and to make the best of every moment, especially when I am surrounded by jolly and smiling young people, as is always my policy!'

'Don't encourage him, Bobbie, or he will start telling you off colour stories, or about his time when detained at Her Majesty's pleasure for knocking policemen's helmets off by the owner's enclosure at Ascot or something.'

'It's a black lie,' said Uncle Peter, 'It was just the one policeman's helmet, and in my intoxicated state, how could I be expected to notice that there was still a policeman inside it!'

'Come on, Uncle Peter. We can read all about this in your autobiography, which I hope there is no danger of your getting into print any time soon, but for now where is this promised Luton van?'

'Unless I am very much mistaken, here it comes now, with my old pal Shifty, in person, at the wheel.'

Bobby and Rosy looked where he was pointing and caught their first glimpse of the vehicle they intended to use to move their worldly goods across London.

'Blimey!' said Rosy.

'Bit of an eyeful, isn't it,' said Uncle Peter, as with a shudder the enormous old vehicle came to a halt beside them.

As Bobbie looked she could see that one side of the main structure was mostly a dull yellow and the other was grimy white. At the front behind a cracked windscreen, between the sweeping windscreen wipers, although the weather was quite dry, a grinning little man in a flat cap raised a hand in greeting and opened the door.

'Lo, Captain,' said the little man, touching the peak of his cap to Uncle Peter, and with a nod, 'Ladies.'

'Shifty, my dear boy!' said Uncle Peter. 'May I introduce my niece Rosy and her charming friend Bobbie.'

'Stameetcha,' said Shifty, and nodding towards the van, 'hope sokay for you. Plentyaroom in there. Best not to turn the wipers off, though. Stalls if yado, dunno why.'

'I'm sure it will do very well, don't you think so ladies? Splendid Shifty, splendid.'

'Showya howta open tha back,' the little man said and beckoned to them to follow him behind the vast vehicle.

Bobbie saw that there was a roller door which was once sign written but the words of whatever it was advertising had been clumsily covered over with black paint.

'Few givit a bang just 'ere,' said Shifty, demonstrating, 'anda gud heave here, she'll open up. Hold that rope mind, or you'll not geddit shutagen.'

'Fine, fine,' said Uncle Peter. 'No doubt you want to be on your way now girls, I expect you have a busy day ahead. Now Rosy have you bought the ah ...'

'The money? Yes of course Uncle Peter. Fifty pounds. Here you are.'

'Fifty?' said Shifty as Uncle Peter handed him thirty pounds.

'And thirty for you Shifty, as agreed. And that deals with the other money you owe me, as well, Rosy.' Uncle Peter gave Rosy a meaningful look, and taking her arm moved away from the van.

'"Tincture" in the two thirty will be the temporary custodian of this twenty pounds, and I confidently predict collecting a good bonus on the investment when the race is run, so that we can regard my introductory commission for finding you this van as paid in full.'

'You old rogue, Uncle Peter! Auntie May sent you out without any money again, then?'

'I'm afraid so. Loveliest woman you could hope to meet, my wife, of course, but doesn't like to think of me funding even the ripest tip on the turf, so she keeps the necessary firmly clutched to her ample bosom.'

Bobbie could see what Rosy liked about this old buster. He was quite a character.

'Pretty hot tip actually. I have it straight from the stable cat. Tincture should walk this race. Make an investment on it's nose without delay, is my advice.'

'No thanks, Uncle Peter. We had better be going now. Thank you for sorting out the van. Shall I drive first, Bobbie?'

-ooOOoo-

Chapter 20

'**Y**es Geoff, I do think it is time we went,' Janet was standing in the hall waiting. 'We promised Bobbie we would help her settle in and we need to get over there. You said yourself that London traffic can be dreadful, even on a Saturday.'

'Just coming, Janet,' called Geoff from the kitchen. 'Got a little moving-in present to take …'

'What have you got there?' Janet eyed the large brown paper carrier bag suspiciously.

'Doughnuts,' said Geoff sheepishly. 'To keep the busy workers going. I've got teabags, coffee, sugar and milk too. And a bottle of wine, of course.'

Janet smiled in-spite of herself.

'Oh come on then, you soppy old sausage!'

'Sausages? That's an idea. We could pick some up on

the way, so they have got something for tea.'

-ooO0oo-

It took a while, but eventually David returned from the pub with the three burly rugby players he had talked into helping them move.

These lads had turned up on time, but as there was no sign of Bobbie and Rosy with the van, they had taken the opportunity to slide off to the pub while there was nothing for them to do.

As the old van rattled its way down the road with the windscreen wipers on, and wisps of steam rising up from the bonnet, they were at least in place in time to start loading it.

-ooO0oo-

The dustbin was almost full of the straw they had swept out of the back of the rusty old van. Its normal work seemed to be delivering bales and feed for horses, given what they found in the back of it, when eventually they convinced the roller door to open.

'Coo, there's a great big hole along the seam there where you can see the road!' exclaimed David as the last of the straw was swept out of a corner.

'Best put a blanket or something over that before we load up,' said Simon, one of the rugby players. 'We don't want to lose half the smaller bits before we get there.'

'Er, guys. I think you should see this,' said Bobbie who was standing at the front of the van.

Now that the old vehicle had juddered to a halt and the engine was switched off, there were clouds of steam rising from the bonnet and, if you listened, a hissing noise from somewhere in the works.

Ginger, another of the rugby players, had the bonnet up in a second.

'Got any eggs?' he asked.

'That's not funny. This is no time to be thinking about boiling eggs!' snapped Rosy.

'No really,' said Ginger blushing red as once again Bobbie caught him admiring her profile. 'There is a leak in the radiator, I think. You can use eggs to block it temporarily if you drop them in the hot water.'

'Good gracious,' said Bobbie. 'I've never heard of that!'

'I'm on it,' said David and set off at a lumbering run for the convenience store on the corner of the road.

-ooO0oo-

Rosy and David's angry little landlord had agreed that they could drop the keys into the corner shop when they had finished moving out.

Bobbie took a turn around the flat with Rosy to make sure nothing had been missed as they prepared to depart.

'At least you will have a bit more room in Kingston,' said Bobbie, who had not seen this place before.

'You are right, Bobbie. Looking at it now I can see how poky it actually is. When we got it I was just so excited to be getting a place of our own that I was blinded to it's inadequacies, I suppose.'

'Oh it is not that bad,' said Bobbie, 'I don't doubt it would have been nice after you got it decorated up.'

'You have seen the kitchen haven't you?' said Rosy. 'The retina melting decorations in there will leave you seeing stars for hours, and to be honest those few cupboards that there are in there really are overdue for a ride in skip.'

'Well, the Kingston place is a bit tired too, to be fair.'

'But at least there is plenty of elbow room ... and two bedrooms. And the landlords are at least human.'

'I like the Patels. They are a sweet old couple.'

'I agree, I'm sure we will be happy there, and the commute to work from Kingston really isn't that much different.'

'Better be making a move then, Rosy.'

-oo0Ooo-

Ginger had purchased a five litre bottle of water from the corner shop when David dropped the key off.

'I think the eggs have worked, but just in case we have to have some water to top up the radiator.'

'How did you know about that trick?' asked David.

'My dad likes tinkering with classic cars and is always having to mend them.'

'Has he got a classic car, then?'

'Er, he collects them actually. There are four in our garage in Roehampton and he has about another three or so scattered about in various garages being restored or just being stored.'

'I had no idea,' said David. 'I thought he worked in insurance in the City.'

'He is a hedge fund manager actually, and he loves his big boys toys. He has got all sorts of things, including an old racing Bentley in bits, and now I come to think about it he has an earlier version of your friend Bobbie's little sports car too, all souped up for racing.'

'I expect Bobbie would like to see that. She loves her little car with a passion.'

'Really? Do you think if I asked her she might like to ...' Ginger was blushing deeply.

'So long as she could take her boyfriend, Pedro, along too, I expect.'

'Oh,' said Ginger, and that was pretty much all he said until they reached the outskirts of Kingston-on-

Thames, when the old van decided to produce steam from under the bonnet once more.

-ooOOoo-

Pedro had spent the morning packing and then cleaning the flat.

He was hot, but pleased that as far as he was able, he was ready.

A glance out of the window told him the old van, wheezing and steaming as it came to a shuddering halt, and David and Rosy's car were outside.

'We might need more eggs,' Ginger was saying as they tumbled up the stairs with the first packing cases.

'Eggs? What needing the eggs?' asked Pedro as Bobbie, pausing only to plant a kiss on his cheek, explained what had been going on. 'Why not the car bits place round a the corner … maybe they sell the plug.'

'Is there a car bits place round the corner?' asked Ginger. 'Is it far?'

'Not the far, no,' said Pedro. 'We walk there two minutes. I show?'

'Well, you might as well go now if you are going to,' said Rosy. 'Then you will be back to help with the heavy stuff, when we have got the little boxes in.'

'Right,' said Ginger. 'If they have got it, there is special stuff in a little bottle you can pour in the radiator which will fix it.'

'Clever,' said David. 'What's it made of?'

'Eggs, probably,' laughed Ginger.

-ooOOoo-

The exhausting business of carrying things up and down stairs was repeated when they got to the Docklands flat, although Bobbie claimed the right to behave like a princess riding up and down in the tiny lift, sometimes carrying hardly anything at all.

The enormous van was too tall to fit through the roller door at the back of the building but Rosy's car fitted easily in the space, even though Bobbie had parked her little sports car in pride of place, right in the middle of the garage.

'Look. My dear little sports car looks so tiny in all that space!' she enthused. 'I suppose I'll have to keep it clean now it lives inside!'

They had to re-arrange things somewhat when Geoff and Janet arrived in their Jaguar. But although the Jaguar protruded a little, and the roller door on the building could not be shut; and the big old van still had to sit half on and half off the pavement outside, the potential for parking tickets on the yellow lines was minimised as the van just about fitted across the wide area with dropped kerbs which designating their private entrance. Geoff spent some time conducting operations to tuck the cars away and eventually Janet, riding down in the little lift, had to tell him to stop messing about and come and help.

Taking a break, they had just sat down with a refreshing cup of tea and one of Geoff's doughnuts, when Bobbie's phone rang.

It was Nurse Emma, from the hospital in Scotland.

-ooO0oo-

Chapter 21

Bobbie went straight to the hospital when she arrived in Scotland and met her mother as she climbed out of a taxi outside.

They went up to the ward together and the nurse on the desk by the entrance asked if the Staff Nurse could have a word before they went in, and showed them into the little room with the armchairs.

'She won't be a moment,' she said, and closed the door behind her.

The Staff Nurse was accompanied by a slightly built doctor who was clutching a clipboard, and who turned on what he obviously thought was an empathetic smile, as he took a seat.

Bobbie's heart was in her mouth as she waited for them to speak.

'You are Mrs and Miss Bassington, Miss Bassington's

172

niece and er ..?' enquired the doctor apologetically.

'Sister-in-law,' explained Bobbie's mother, and the little man nodded and made a note on his clipboard.

'I'm afraid I must tell you that Caroline is very unwell.'

'Oh,' said Bobbie.

'I'm very sorry. We have established that she has had a stroke and she has lost some function as a result. She now finds communication very difficult, although we are all most impressed that until very recently she had still been typing little messages on her phone sometimes. That is quite remarkable. But I have to tell you that her mental processes are now shutting down, and she may not be entirely aware of what is going on around her.'

Bobbie clutched her mother's hand as the doctor and the staff nurse became blurry, and the tears that were starting to fill her eyes began to escape and roll down her cheeks.

'I'm very sorry to say that she is sedated now so that we can control her breathing a little better. You should not expect her to be able to be able communicate, although we think she may know you are there. Perhaps you could hold her hand. '

The Staff Nurse shifted in her chair and the little man continued with an embarrassed cough.

'I'm sorry to say that her body is beginning to shut

down and I'm afraid that we are now quite close to the end. I can assure you that she is very comfortable and not in any pain, and we will continue to hydrate her, but other than that, there is nothing we can do.'

Bobbie let out an involuntary sniff and took the tissues the nurse was handing her. She wanted to scream or cry out of course, but she managed to stifle the urge.

'Would you like to see her now?' said the nurse.

-oo0Ooo-

Caroline passed away later that night when Bobbie and her mother had taken a break from their bedside vigil and visited the hospital's bleak and uncomfortable cafe.

The nurse on duty who discovered the body was shocked to notice that the screen was lit up on the mobile phone still in her hand and Caroline had managed to type *'drugs paid s'* on the screen before she died.

Bobbie knew what it meant immediately, and Caroline was right. It was the last piece of the jigsaw and Caroline had fought to stay alive long enough to help Bobbie work it out.

It meant that Paul Stevens had been paid with the drugs from the drop, out at sea, for finding and handing over Eoin O'Grady.

That is where the drugs went.

-ooo0oo-

Detective Sergeant Mike Rowbotham offered his condolences for her loss and told Bobbie that if she was up to it, he would like to tell her some news.

'After what you told us about the Girl Sue we arrested Finn Stevens, who is Paul Stevens father, by the way,' he said. 'We have impounded the Girl Sue and the forensic boys are taking a look at it.'

'I see,' said Bobbie. 'What about the other people who were on the boat. The note on the Lady Irene said "Stevens (3)", which I took to mean there were three of them; and is it really possible that Finn Stevens would be able to handle a big boat like the Girl Sue on his own?'

'I'm told that the Girl Sue would usually have a crew of three or four, and although I'm no expert in these matters, I would have thought such a big boat would certainly need more than one person to handle it. At present, though, we have no idea where Paul Stevens is and Finn Stevens is being very obstructive. He says he knows nothing about anyone called Eoin O'Grady and when we reminded him of the story of the weapons on the Eksund, he said ... hang on, I have it here ... "Time all that sort of thing was buried with the dead and forgotten about. No need to rake it all up again." He also said there was nobody else on the Girl Sue apart from his son Paul and there was nobody on the Lady Irene when they came across it out at sea. He said he had tried to report it's position to the Coastguard, but that atmospheric conditions disrupted his radio communications, so his report may not have been received.'

'Well, it seems much more likely that he took Paul off the Lady Irene, after they shot O'Grady, don't you think. But where did he take him after that?'

'Finn would have known that satellites can track boat movements so he did not try to fudge that one, he said he took Paul to Liverpool and hasn't seen him since. The Girl Sue was seen at a marina near there, so there was no point denying that it had been to Liverpool.'

'I don't suppose the Liverpool police ...'

'No, no sign of him, I'm afraid, and we can't prove he was on the boat when it got there, anyway.'

'So the other crew and possibly the people who murdered Eoin O'Grady probably got taken to Liverpool as well.'

'It would be reasonable to assume so. We have charged Finn Stevens with being an accessory to murder, which will keep him in custody for now. He already has a Police record from many years ago involving pub brawls, but nothing more recently. Ballistics checked him over and could find none of the minute traces that gunshots leave, so it probably wasn't him who actually did the shooting.'

'What about those satellite images, don't they show anybody else on board either boat?'

'I'm afraid the images are too indistinct, Bobbie. Taken from too far away and it was raining quite heavily and was stormy at the time.'

'So would you agree that the reason Paul Stevens left Ballybunion a day early and did not play the round of golf he had booked and paid for, was because the body was found on the beach?'

'Very probably. There is something else you may as well know about that too. We think Eoin O'Grady was tied up and thrown into the sea without disguising the body or removing any of his identification from his pockets because the killers knew the body would wash up sooner or later somewhere along that stretch of coast and could be immediately identified. That would demonstrate to anyone he knew, or who knew who he was, that these killers will seek revenge without mercy if they are crossed, no matter how long it takes.'

'Nasty,' said Bobbie.

'Yes, but we think the body washed ashore a bit sooner that they thought it would, and that is why Paul Stevens ran.'

'But what was he doing there anyway? I thought you said he had been dropped off in Liverpool.'

'That was quite difficult for us to understand too. We think he might have been dropped off somewhere before they got to Liverpool, in Ireland, and was driven to the Ballybunion hotel in time for the body to be washed up. We are requesting more satellite imagery to see if we can prove that. The tides and currents in that area mean that the body was only likely to wash up on one of about three bits of beach or in a small bay, given where they put it in the sea, and it wasn't weighted down so it wouldn't just sink. Someone like Finn Stevens, as a skipper of a sea-going boat, would know all about tides and currents and would have been able to work out pretty accurately where it would come ashore. The only thing they miscalculated was how quickly it would wash up.'

'Paul Stevens took pictures of the body when it was on the beach. At first Pauline and I assumed that, although it was a bit macabre, it was because he was a journalist and it was for his paper. But there was more to that, wasn't there …'

'Yes, Bobbie. Very perceptive. Maybe you should be a detective. Those photos were to prove to whoever was paying him that the body had washed up and where.'

'And probably,' Bobbie said, 'to get them to release the money to pay him.'

'I should point out,' the detective said, 'that this could be any one of a number of groups made up of the fanatics left out in the cold when the break up of the recognised body of the IRA as a fighting force took place. With ruthless people like these, proving that they have done the killing is every bit as important as doing the killing itself.'

'Do you think Paul Stevens did the shooting?'

'No. Do you?'

'No. But who did?'

'I'm afraid we may never know who pulled the trigger that ended Eoin O'Grady's life, but we will keep looking as long as the fanatical terrorists who caused this mayhem are still out there, seeking revenge on those who crossed them.'

'Can I use those last words in my article? That is rather good and will round it off nicely.'

'Un-attributed?'

'Naturally. From an 'anonymous source'.'

'OK.'

'Do you know why Paul Stevens got the sack from the Irish Times?'

'Yes.'

'Go on …'

'All right, I suppose I might as well tell you … it was because their HR department belatedly found out that he was an IRA sympathiser and had been arrested once on a march.'

'Why belatedly?'

The policeman sighed. 'Because I'm afraid it took the Police Records department over three months to respond to the newspaper's HR people, when they sent in their standard background check request for information at the time they offered Paul Stevens a job.'

'I don't suppose you want me to quote that bit, do you?'

'I'd rather you didn't. Look Bobbie, I really am sorry to hear about Caroline,' said DS Rowbotham. 'Please do let me know when and where the funeral is.'

-ooOOoo-

Chapter 22

Bobbie finished writing up the story, and as she prepared to submit it to Button and Cohen, her favoured news agency, she added a personal tribute.

"We may never know who actually pulled the trigger of the gun that killed Eoin O'Grady, but the rump of the fanatical terrorists who caused such mayhem are still out there seeking revenge on those who crossed them. At least today we can sleep a little easier in our beds, in the knowledge that the handful of investigative journalists who tirelessly track this sort of thing sometimes succeed in helping the authorities to bring these criminals to book. It took Caroline Bassington thirty six years to finish the story of Eoin O'Grady, following the capture of the gun running boat the Eksund by the French police in 1987. But long after others had forgotten about it Caroline painstakingly pieced the facts together. It was what she did, all her life, right up until the very last minute. She will be sorely missed by those who knew her and all those

she helped throughout her life."

She sighed, pressed 'send' and picked up a well thumbed travel brochure. She had kept it since her first trip there, and now started reading once again about the wonders of the better bits of the Costa Blanca, in Spain. She could do with a holiday, she decided.

-ooOOoo-

The story was published around the world and, in the prestigious Metropolitan Journal, it appeared next to a wonderful obituary for Caroline Bassington, written and produced by Button and Cohen, the international news agency, for whom she so often wrote. It finished by giving details of how to make contributions to the charity running Hackdoone House which Caroline set up and for which, at her funeral, those invited had been asked for a financial contribution, instead of sending flowers.

As Bobbie finished reading it, and caught sight of a tempting advertisement for a beach holiday on the facing page as she laid it aside, her phone rang in her pocket.

Coincidentally it was her friend Henry who worked for Button and Cohen, and he breathlessly told her that the wires were alive with a story about new luxury executive aircraft being sold with potentially faulty imported components by a company in France. The company, Henry told her, was also under investigation for tax fraud, and nobody could find the Chief Executive.

'Sounds like one for you to investigate, Bobbie,' he said.

'I'll check it out,' said Bobbie. Perhaps the holiday was going to have to wait.

-ooO0oo-

Epilogue

'**W**e have apprehended Paul Stevens, Bobbie,' said Detective Sergeant Mike Rowbotham.

'Fantastic! Where did you catch him? Liverpool?'

'No, Plymouth. And we were a bit lucky really. The police there got a call from a boat brokerage who were worried because a customer was trying to buy a secondhand sea-going motor cruiser with cash, and thought it might be money laundering. They arrested him, and because the address on his driving licence is County Kerry we got to hear about it.'

'Well at least he has been caught.'

'Yes, although I'd rather you kept the luck bit to yourself.'

'Of course, no problem.'

'You remember the Lady Irene?'

'Yes?'

'Well the owner was a Conor Doherty ...'

'The container ship magnate and Parish Councillor from a posh suburb of Liverpool.'

'That's the one. When Paul Stevens thought we were going to cut him a deal he told us that he knew the drugs that they pulled out of the sea were delivered to this Doherty. Doherty, it now emerges, is involved in wholesale drug supply in Liverpool, and the local police have had him on their radar for some time. He has been arrested too. But there is a bit more to this, you remember that Stevens took pictures of the body on the beach and we hypothesised that it was to get the people who commissioned the shooting to release the money?'

'Yes ...'

'Well it transpires that it was Doherty's wife who wanted the pictures and gave the go-ahead to her husband to release the money.'

'His wife!'

'Yes, and this is the good bit ... We have been working with the English police for years and years trying to track down a woman who was once a big wheel in the more outspoken end of Irish politics, but seemed to have dropped off the radar completely. She had some pretty hard line views and having found no trace of her, we wondered if she had fled abroad or even been bumped off. But, living under an assumed name and now with a whole new identity, it turns out she is none other than Doherty's wife! She only married Doherty six months ago, but when she was politically active, in the 1980's, and called herself Mary O'Toole, she is known to have organised marches, and possibly direct action. At that time she was in a relationship with Paul's father, Finn Stevens. Needless to say she has been arrested too.'

'But Doherty occasionally rented the Lady Irene to Eoin O'Grady. Didn't he know about his history with the Eksund?'

'Apparently not Bobbie, or perhaps it didn't mean anything to him. It was only when Paul Stevens got involved and Doherty's new wife became aware that Eoin O'Grady was paying to rent the Lady Irene occasionally, that they made the connection and this all kicked off.'

'And now you have caught her too. A pretty spectacular outcome, I'd say.'

'Better than we could have hoped for when the body washed up on the beach, I have to say. Thank you, Bobbie. All this started with you and your aunt picking up on this story, after all.'

'And all that started with a little old lady walking her dog. Rather a nice little old lady, as it happens. And Buster of course.'

'Who?'

'Buster. He found the body.'

-oo0Ooo-

As the weather was dry and warm, Bobbie drove her little sports-car down to Dorking with the top down. The experience was exhilarating and helped to clear her mind.

As she parked the car when she arrived at Hackdoone House, and was untying and shaking loose her long auburn hair, John Parish appeared in the doorway in his wheelchair and welcomed her inside.

'Hello Bobbie,' he said. 'Come on in. I have the information you want, I think. There is nobody using the office, so we can talk in there.'

'I'm sorry if this put you to any trouble, John,' said Bobbie.

'Not at all. I enjoyed giving the old grey matter a work out as I tried to remember the facts and get the sequence of events in the right order,' smiled John. 'Now before we start, would you like a coffee or anything?'

'I'd rather you told me what you have remembered first, and then perhaps a small cider …'

'Certainly! An excellent idea, Bobbie.'

Shifting his weight in his wheelchair, John pulled a

notepad from a pocket and began his story.

'Mary O'Toole was a horrible piece of work,' he stated. 'One of those shrill, aggressive Irish women who shout rather than talk, and you always felt she was going to start throwing things at any moment. She had very extreme views and always threatened to bring down Armageddon on all our heads if the Catholic side of the Irish debate did not triumph. I confess I was rather scared of her.'

'But you interviewed her twice?'

'Yes. The first time was just the usual political rant and gave me nothing new, but on the second occasion, which was just after the cinema bombing your aunt and I attended, she was a bit more forthcoming.'

'I had a feeling the cinema bombing might come up,' said Bobbie.

'It was our link to Eoin O'Grady, although as it turned out, nobody actually showed up for the meeting. We suspected Mary O'Toole and her ghastly IRA paramilitaries had guessed that we planned to meet someone connected with the ship, the Eksund, there and she wanted to be there to catch them. I couldn't prove it, but I'm sure she was planning to break into that meeting, and she admitted she was nearby when the explosion took place. She claimed it was her, rather than us, that the Ulster Freedom Fighters were after when they blew up the old cinema. It might well have been. That would have been quite possible. If the

UFF knew she was going to be there, knocking her off would have been pretty prize for violent thugs on the opposing Protestant side of the political divide, like them.'

'But you still went to meet with her, even though you knew she might want to do you harm?'

'She came mob handed to that second meeting, but there was nothing she could do as we had an Army escort.'

'Was my Auntie Caroline there?'

'No, just me and a couple of other fellows from the American and English press, and the Army boys, of course.'

'I see. Was there anybody else there?'

'There were a couple of heavies lurking nearby in black balaclavas of course, and she arrived in a minibus driven by her boyfriend, Finn Stevens.'

'How did you know he was her boyfriend?'

'Body language. We had heard rumours about his relationship with her and, as they were walking towards the municipal playground where we planned to meet, she tripped and linked her arm through his to steady herself.'

'Cozy.'

'How much do you know about Finn Stevens, Bobbie.'

'Not nearly enough, if I'm honest.'

John turned the pages of his notebook.

'Finn Stevens ran a construction company that did office and shop fit-outs, in London mostly. At that time the construction industry was rife with IRA supporters, and it was not at all unusual to see shady characters turning up on building sites shaking plastic buckets which they used to collect cash donations from the workers, sometimes using intimidation. Finn Stevens company worked all over London, and the British suspected that he was a major fund-raiser, but could never pin anything on him.'

'Did he live in London?'

'Some of the time. He also owned a farm out in the wilds in Ireland where it is rumoured the IRA met to plot, and where it is thought Mary O'Toole might have lived at one time. She completely vanished though, and most people thought she had skipped the country when it got a bit hot for her. There is one odd thing though ...'

'Go on.'

'Well, Mary O'Toole was a short, skinny, busy little woman, and all the pictures of her show her wearing tight black jeans, which were fashionable at that time. When she came to meet us she was wearing a dress and had put on quite a lot of weight. I wondered if she was pregnant.'

'Oh,' said Bobbie. 'You don't think she is Paul Steven's mother do you?'

'No. The time scale is all wrong. How old would you say Paul Stevens is ... late twenties?'

'Yes, probably.'

'Well, I was interviewing Mary in 1987.'

'That can't be right then. Maybe that was the start of her attempt to change her appearance before she disappeared.'

'That is a possibility, I suppose. I hadn't thought of that. But, as I was saying, Finn Stevens went on to marry another Irish girl who worked in his office. She was killed in a road accident on their twenty first wedding anniversary. I remember that because she apparently drove into a tree on a quiet country road with nobody else about, in fine weather in the middle of the afternoon. It seemed a bit suspicious, but again nothing was ever proved.'

'And she gave birth to Paul?'

'Yes. It is her name on the birth certificate.'

'What happened to Finn Stevens later on?'

'It seems he just continued running his building contracting firm and didn't seem to be involved in any more political activity. He must have done quite well at that though if he managed to buy a share of that pretentious boat you were telling me about.'

'Either that or he was running drugs from drop-off points in the Atlantic off the Irish coast with it.'

'That is an investigation for another day, I suspect, Bobbie. For now I should think he is going to be locked up for some time.'

'You are right, of course. But at least the authorities will know where to find him.'

'True. Now how about that little glass of cider, young lady?'

-ooO0Ooo-

Bobbie met the Funeral Director at the main entrance to Kensington Cemetery by the chapel as agreed. He had bought a note with the number of the lot and a map to help them find it.

He had also bought Caroline's ashes in a discrete box.

It took them quite a few minutes to find the correct location and then a little longer to find what they were looking for, but eventually Bobbie was able to add Caroline's ashes to those of her daughter, Nicola Ann, who had lived for just one day.

-ooO0Ooo-

Granted, it wasn't the Costa Blanca, but ten days in Caroline's cottage ... which, of course, was now her cottage … in Scotland, with Pedro, Geoff and Janet was still a holiday of sorts for Bobbie.

She unpacked with a sigh of contentment and prepared to go downstairs.

'It's really pretty,' Janet called up. 'And I bet there are loads of fish in there,' added Geoff, 'Come on Bobbie, join us for a walk along the river!'

'On my way,' said Bobbie.

Geoff, she knew, was looking forward to next week, when Bobbie went home with Janet and he was joined by Retired Colonel Cyril Duncan-Browne for a week of fly fishing on the river, just down the road.

But she was looking forward to the shopping trip she and Janet had planned for *this* week, and she had already mapped out a route around the most promising dress shops in her mind. She wanted a new outfit, or perhaps two, for Toenail's big weekend party, which was now approaching rapidly.

She grabbed her phone from the bed and noticed a text message had arrived.

It was from Pauline Patrick in Ballybunion … 'Buster says thanks for the bone!' it read.

THE END.

-ooO0oo-

****

Notes: The story of the capture of the Eksund and it's skipper, Adrian Hopkins with his massive cargo of weapons bound for the IRA from Libya in 1987 is true, (although Eoin O'Grady is a fictional invention for this book), as is the description of the 'Ulster Freedom Fighters' bombing of the cinema in Dublin on 7/2/1987, but all the events and characters described around that in this book are fictional.

The author acknowledges the references to those incidents in the Belfast Telegraph and the Irish Times obituaries published in 2015, and also thanks Susanne Fuchs, writing in Curiosity Magazine about life on a container ship, as the inspiration behind part of this story. All other incidents, characters and references are purely fictional.

Bob Able:

If you like Bob Able's distinctive writing style and would like to read more of his work, here is a little more information .....

Bob Able is a writer of fiction, thrillers and memoirs and describes himself as a 'part-time expat' splitting his time between coastal East Anglia in England, and the Costa Blanca in Spain.

He writes with a lighthearted touch and does not use graphic descriptions of sex or violence in his books, that is not his style. He prefers to leave that sort of thing to the reader's imagination.

Other Bobby Bassington Stories include:

'**Bobbie And The Spanish Chap**',
'**Bobbie And The Crime-Fighting Auntie**', and
'**Bobbie And The Wine Trouble**'.
Bobbie makes her first appearance in '**Double Life Insurance**'.

'**Spain Tomorrow**', is a Bestseller and was the first book in his popular and amusing memoir series. It was the **third most popular travel book on Amazon** in late 2020 and with its sequel, '**More Spain Tomorrow**' it continues to attract many good reviews and an appreciative audience in Europe, the United Kingdom, the USA and beyond.

His fictional novels include '**Double Life Insurance**' (with Bobbie Bassington fresh out of university but already uncovering an international fraud), '**No Point Running**' (set in the world of horse racing in the 1970's ... see below), '**The Menace Of Blood**' (which is about inheritance, not gore) and the sequel '**No Legacy of Blood**', and are fast-paced engaging thrillers, with a touch of romance and still with that gentle, signature Bob Able humour.

His semi-fictional memoir '**Silke The Cat, My Story**', written with his friend and wine merchant, Graham Austin and Silke the Cat herself, is completely different. Silke is a real cat, she lives today in the Costa Blanca, and her adventures, which she recounts in this amusing book, really happened (also available as an audio book).

All Bob's books are available from Amazon as

paperbacks or ebooks.

-oo0Ooo-

An extract from 'No Point Running', Bob Able's thriller set in the 1970's: -

'Well, life was simpler in 1978, I suppose you could say. No mobile phones or internet or any of that rot, and Amazon was still just a river. Mind you, that didn't stop me, as a former car thief and telephone sanitiser getting involved, as a guest at a country house with the horse racing set, and almost getting murdered, amongst the highest levels of society; twice.'

Chapter 1

On Tuesday, at 17:15, I died.

No doubt the swarm of nurses, doctors and sundry hangers-on checked all the pipes, wires and tubes and, when the heart monitor confirmed my status, they were galvanised into action.
After some unseemly pummelling and the injection of stimulants, at 17:32, according to the notes on the clipboard at the end of my bed, I breathed again. It had

been close, but for some, not close enough.

Allow me to explain.

I'm not actually a bad lad but I have, how shall we say, found the straight and narrow path a little constraining at times. My employment, such as it was, for the last couple of years had mostly involved motor cars, and their removal. But not just any cars, I only procured high end stuff, to order, and for immediate shipment abroad.

The owners of the luxurious or sometimes fast and flashy vehicles hadn't actually handed me the keys and sent me on my way with a cheery wave, so some upset was to be expected if I was disturbed in my work.

Josh Pindar was a case in point. He had made his money bookmaking and his Bentley Continental, with his pretentious JSP 123 number plate, was testament to his success. but when I took it for a spin and accidentally sold it, he became quite cross and decided to seek me out.

There were to be no police searches for Josh though. He didn't want any flatfooted bluebottles eyeing up his operation, so he decided on a different strategy.
He put the word out that he was looking for a replacement for the Bentley, by fair means or foul, and at the earliest possible date. To that end Big Mel, one of his associates, picked up on the request and contacted Tinker Pete who it just so happened occasionally commissioned my services.

Of course it wasn't Tinker Pete I was working for when I nicked Josh's first Bentley and he had no idea of the connection. It was just bad luck that Tinker Pete was the person Big Mel approached with quite an exacting brief as to the colour and specification required and Tinker Pete engaged me to fulfil the order.

I'd arranged to meet Big Mel in a bar by Wimbledon station at a certain date and time and innocently enough explained that, if I could find one, actually pinching the motor would be no problem as I had made a comparable acquisition just a week ago for one of my overseas clients.

I thought Big Mel's reaction was a little unusual in that his eyes widened and a muscle in his ample jaw twitched when I dropped this pearl of wisdom, but I thought nothing of it at the time.

Big Mel bought me another drink and asked me to study the specification of the car his boss required and I, foolishly I now realise, expressed my surprise that it was the absolute spit of the one I had recently lifted.
'Popular choice, it seems.' I added as Mel excused himself to make a call from the phone box outside.

I remember him coming back to the table, and that nerve in his jaw jumping, but that was it until I woke up in the hospital bed.

Having counted my limbs, felt my teeth with my tongue and tried, painfully, to move my arms and legs, I established that I was somewhat bruised, but broadly still in one piece. My head, however, had gained a solid attachment to an unseen jackhammer and I decided, then and there, that a change of career might be an attractive proposition.

I was good at what I did, however, and had never troubled the police with my activities so I was somewhat surprised to find, as focus returned and I could make out more of my surroundings, that a uniformed female police officer was standing by my bed.

The significance of her presence became clearer when she said,
'Ah, he's coming round, 'and to me, 'Have you any idea how this happened to you?'

A nurse, who I had not noticed until this point, hustled her aside and said something along the lines that this was not the time for questions, and would she please wait in the hall.

As my faculties began to return, I noticed that this efficient nurse was strikingly pretty. She was bustling about checking the monitors and so forth when she said, 'So how are you feeling?'
Somewhat painfully a kernel of a thought was trying to make its presence known in my aching head.

In my profession, if you can call it that, it is unwise to carry any form of identification on the person and, as the meeting with Big Mel did not involve using my tools, they remained at home when I met him.
Could it be, I wondered....

I tried a tentative 'Where am I? 'and the nurse, who had her rather shapely back to me at the time, turned around.

'Now you just try to relax, 'she was saying, 'What's your name by the way?'

The idea that had been tapping on my cerebral cortex demanding attention burst into life in my head.

'My, my name? 'I mumbled, 'I, what …. oh my head!'

I added a couple of groans for good measure and left it at that, there being no apparent need to rush these things.

But things were moving fast anyway, and here was a white coated individual, complete with stethoscope and clip board who had questions of his own for me.

All in all, these interludes helped with my ideas for a change of career. Could acting be my destiny, or perhaps selling life insurance? It certainly seemed the nurse, the doctor and now the lady police officer were eating up my little show and were hungry for more.

Eventually they explained to me that I was scraped up from behind the bins at the back of the bar in Wimbledon and deposited here by persons unknown who had the use of the company ambulance.
The chef, or similar, at the bar had discovered me as he collected his bicycle at the end of the lunchtime shift, and called the authorities.

As I gathered this information I expressed surprise at every turn and, hopefully without over doing it, continued to deny all knowledge of my address, reason for splattering the bins with a good deal of my vital claret, or for that matter giving my name.

Various doctors came and went, including one in a suit who asked me all sorts of leading questions and was, I suspect, sent to see if I was making up the memory loss thing.
I was careful and, jackhammer allowing, thoughtful in my responses and it seems I got away with it …

You can find details of how to buy 'No Point

Running' and all Bob's books at:
www.amazon.com/author/bobable

Contact:

bobable693@gmail.com

www.amazon.com/author/bobable

Or just enter **Bob Able books** on the Amazon site and the full list should appear.

He also has a website, but, 'having the technical ability of a teaspoon', hates updating it so don't expect too much!
www.bobable693.wixsite.com/spain-tomorrow

Disclaimer:

You may like to know that Bob Able supports 'The Big C', Norfolk's Cancer Charity, who have helped Bob with his own cancer battle and who do great practical work to help cancer victims and promote research. Find out more at: www.big-c.co.uk

Printed in Great Britain
by Amazon